Ingo Blum

BRIDGET KNOTTERFIELD

AND THE HICCUP FANTASY TREES

illustrated by
Svetlana Janev

First Edition

Illustrated by Svetlana Janev

Book Design: Bea Balint

ISBN 978-3-947410-46-0

For Melanie

So Nature keeps the reverent frame

With which her years began,

And all her signs and voices shame

The prayerless heart of man.

John Greenleaf Whittier

Contents

A Nightly Encounter

Eight-year-old Bridget Knotterfield loved trees. She liked to climb in them, sit in them, and build tree houses. She loved their swaying branches, their solid trunks, and the wind singing in their leaves. She could not stand any living trees being damaged or cut. Her favorite season was spring when the trees became brilliant green again after the dreary winter time.

Bridget was a tiny girl with curly brown hair, brown eyes, and a vivid smile. Her family and most of her friends called her Bridge.

Indeed, she was a special girl. Everybody said that— her mother and father, her six-year-old brother, Tom, her classmates and friends, and her neighbors. In short, everybody who knew her thought she was special.

First, it was because of her love for trees. But then it was because of the hiccups she got when she was anxious. Bridget hated these hiccups. She could not do anything to stop it, and sometimes she was very sad about it. Sometimes at school, she had to sit in the back row, instead of with her friends, because her hiccups were too loud. Sometimes, she couldn't eat her lunch because her hiccups were too strong.

Bridget lived with her parents and her brother in a small town in Canada. Behind their house was a grassy field that nobody used. Behind it stood a dense forest with a small path leading into it. During daytime, Tom and Bridget played between the tall trees. Tom was still very small for his age, with messy brown hair and a cheeky smile.

Bridget always loved playing under the trees. Her favorite game was hide and seek. Most of the time their dog, Towser, a German sheepdog, joined them. The kids loved Towser, but when they played hide and seek, he often smelled the one hiding. No hiding place was secret for more than five minutes before Towser found it.

However, Tom and Bridget also liked to build tree men in the grassy field. A tree man was built with pieces of trees. It always looked pretty crazy and building it was a lot of fun. Mostly a big tree trunk was the body, while the arms and feet were made of branches, roots, and twigs. On top, they put a funny looking head their father carved from a root. Their tree man had two painted blue eyes, a long wooden nose like Pinocchio's, and a big red smiling mouth. Finally they chose an old hat from their grandma to put on the root-head and yes—the tree man was ready!

One night in late spring, it happened.

Bridget was watching the tree man from her room on the first floor of the house. The tree man stood in the field, facing towards her room.

Bridget gave a start. It seemed as though the tree man's eyes had shifted to stare straight at her! Of course, that could not be the case. Bridget watched the tree man until it became too dark to see his eyes. Then she went to bed.

During the night, she was suddenly awoken by a strange noise. *The tree man?* she wondered. She opened her window and fresh piney air drifted in. The moon shone brightly on the tree man, his twiggy fingers white and pale.

The noise, coming from the grass, was a loud howling. Was the tree man brought to life during the night? She heard a snarling and barking. Towser? What was he doing out there?

Bridget decided to find out what was happening.

She closed the window and reached for her dressing gown, finding it easily in the bright moonlight. She tiptoed past the room next to hers, where Tom slept. In the room opposite, her father was snoring. Except for the snore, everything was quiet.

Silently, she went downstairs and opened the main door. Howling and snarling and then a long roar filled her ears. *Did nobody else hear that noise?*

She went a couple of steps towards the field and whispered, "Towser, you there?" She heard whining but could not see him, despite the moonlight. Bridget moved forward until she nearly reached the tree man. She repeated the dog's name several times, but Towser did not appear. Normally, he was very obedient.

Bridget was worried; the whining sounded unhappy. Then, suddenly, she saw Towser behind the tree man. He must have left the house through the dog's door.

But he was not alone.

Actually, he was in a fierce fight with another animal that Bridget did not recognize. Was it a fox? A bear?

No, a bear was bigger. Then she realized—it was a wolf! Yes, it was a huge, strong brindled wolf. She did not really have the time to think what to do. The wolf's teeth glinted in the moonlight.

Hair stood up on Bridget's neck. Her heart hammered.

The trees of the nearby forest suddenly seemed threatening; were more wolves hiding amongst them? Even the tree man threw weird, scary shadows. Bridget stood frozen as the battle between Towser and the monster wolf continued, as they whined and howled terribly. For the first time in her life, Bridget felt an overwhelming fear.

She was face to face with a huge wolf. What would happen if Towser ran away? Or got killed?

She screamed. Her cry rose into the night, shrill and loud and full of fear. It woke up her parents, her brother, and some of the neighbors.

"Bridge, what are you doing out there?" Her father called from the house.

But all Bridget could do was hiccup . . . and hiccup . . . and hiccup.

How to cure a Hiccup?

"Towser had a battle with that wolf to defend the tree man," Bridget's father assumed the next day.

He took Towser to the vet, but the dog was lucky. He only had a couple of bruises and scratches. Obviously, the wolf had not been in the mood to hurt or even kill the dog. The wolf was large enough to do this if he'd wanted to.

"I have never seen a wolf here in this territory," her

mother said, shaking her head.

Mr. Knotterfield added, "They normally stay in the mountains. Even Aunt Claire only saw one last winter. And she is living two days' drive north of here." Aunt Claire was Bridget's mother's sister.

The wolf was a mystery. How did he come all the way south to this place? Did he get lost? Lost from his pack? If so, they had to be very careful not to meet his pack, or him, again.

"Maybe he is still around," Tom said.

"Let's be careful," Mr. Knotterfield said, "but I do not believe he will come again."

"Are you okay, Bridget?" Her mother asked over and over again that day.

Bridget's answer was a loud and crampy *hic*! *Hic!* Her hiccups had not gone away since she gave that cry of panic in the night. She and Tom had not gone out to play in the field that day. They were afraid of the wolf returning, even in daytime. You never knew. *The trees cannot save me from a monster wolf,*

Bridget thought nervously.

Days past without the wolf reappearing. Every evening, Bridget watched the tree man from her bedroom window. The tree man was so alone. Bridget waited to see if his eyes would move again, but they didn't.

Her parents tried to cure her hiccups with popular remedies. We all know them. Bridget had to breathe in and hold her breath for about ten seconds, then breathe out slowly and repeat three or four times. She gargled with iced water and tried to remember a nice day she enjoyed, a meal she ate, or a funny film she watched.

Nothing helped.

Tom laughed sometimes because the hiccups were funny. "Bridge is a hiccup girl! Bridge is a hiccup girl!" he chanted. She stuck out her tongue and finally he got tired of teasing her.

She tried to fight the hiccups alone, but finally she had to see Dr. Brent. He was one of the best doctors in town, and he'd known the Knotterfield family for a long time. Even he could not determine anything different about Bridget's hiccups. "They seem normal," he muttered. He placed a couple of drops of vinegar in Bridget's mouth—*ugh!*—and suggested some simple tricks that she could do on her own.

"Gently compress your chest, this can be achieved by leaning forward," he said.

She leaned.

"Place gentle pressure on your nose while you swallow."

She tried.

"Press your diaphragm gently."

She pressed.

Dr. Brent went to a fruit bowl and grabbed a fresh lemon, sliced it into round pieces, and gave one to Bridget. "Place it on your tongue and suck it like a candy."

She sucked. *Ugh, that was sour!*

Hic, hic, hiccup went Bridget. Dr. Brent sighed heavily through his nose.

The hiccups mainly came during the nights. It was hard to sleep with hiccups. Bridget read books with a flashlight; she looked at pictures of the world's oldest and tallest trees on her phone. Sometimes, Bridget peeked out of her window, with the hair standing up on her arms.

Hic! Hic!

Bridget was exhausted and kept going to sleep in class. Her teacher started writing notes home to her parents. They took her to see Dr. Brent several more times. He tried dozens of different ways to cure the hiccups, and finally, he was successful. "Now she's fit as a fiddle," said Dr. Brent. "It will not come back." He sounded sure.

Her mother agreed, "It was just a normal hiccup caused by being scared of Towser fighting the wolf."

Now Bridget could stay awake in class and bring her slipping grades back up. She'd slept so much she'd got a D in nature studies! Usually, she was top of the class. She was not scared anymore and tried to forget her encounter with Towser and the wolf.

One evening, Tom came and sat beside her bed. "What was it like?" he asked. "The wolf fight?"

"It was terrible. You really want to know?"

"Sure!" he said, but his eyes grew very big.

Bridget told Tom the whole story. After that, Tom liked to sneak to Bridget's room in the evening and look out, but he never saw a wolf.

Bridget and Tom decided it was safe to start playing in the field again. Their neighborhood friends joined them for a game of tag. *The field seems smaller than it did before*, Bridget thought. *Or am I just imagining it?* As she ran around, she had to dodge between trees standing in the grass. Finally, she stopped and gazed upwards. A maple tree, with a pink trunk, dangled red and yellow leaves over her head.

"A blue tree!" shrieked another child. Soon all the

kids were laughing and calling as they noticed that the trees growing into the field were purple, orange, peach, and silver. Soon a big crowd of parents gathered at the edge of the forest. People wondered what was happening.

"What an awesome bunch of trees," one of the kids said.

"Look at this oak tree with a blue trunk. I have never seen that before," said a parent.

People shook their heads in disbelief. How could those trees grow so rapidly?

"They're *fantasy trees*!" cried Tom.

"Yeah, that's what they are. They're fantasy trees!" shouted the other kids. That night, under the covers, Bridget looked at tree pictures on her phone. She looked at Indian trees, African trees, Australian trees . . . but she could not find any trees with all those bright colors. It was another mystery.

Fantasy Trees

"The tree man is gone!" Tom said one morning about a week later.

Straight away the Knotterfield family went to the living room window overlooking the forest. The living room was below Bridget's bedroom. They were still puzzling about the colorful trees. Was it normal for trees to be so bright in the spring?

Possibly, though maybe not with blue trunks like the oak tree. That was indeed strange.

"The tree man is not gone," Mrs. Knotterfield said. "It is behind the firs over there!"

She pointed at a group of blue, yellow, and green firs standing in the grass. Firs can be green and blue, but yellow? They weren't big but had wide branches that completely encircled the tree man.

"They weren't there yesterday," Bridget said.

"I don't know," muttered her father uneasily.

"I am sure they weren't," said Bridget.

She did not admit that, last night, she'd seen a shadow by the forest. She did not tell her parents that this had made her hiccup. She'd thought at first that the shadows were the monster wolf again. It had turned out not to be, but by then it was too late; she'd already hiccupped.

"These firs look like Christmas trees," Tom giggled.

Mrs. Knotterfield stared at them with a worried

frown. "What's going on?" she wondered.

Bridget stared at the tree man standing in the firs. *This is scary,* she thought. Where did those firs come from? Then she saw the shadow again in the dense forest beyond the field. She only glimpsed it for a second, and then it was gone again. *The monster wolf*! Bridget suddenly felt a grumble in her stomach. She gasped.

Hic, hic!

"Oh no, not again!" her father said. There was a sudden humming and cracking from the far side of the new firs. Out of nowhere, another fir, this one red, appeared from the soil. It grew rapidly in front of the other firs and hid the tree man completely. "That is unbelievable!"

"That is simply impossible!" Mrs. Knotterfield shook her head.

"How can a tree grow so fast?" Tom wondered.

Nobody had an answer to that.

"The trees are very near now," her father whispered.

Bridget said nothing. She was still looking for the monster wolf at the edge of the woods. But the only animal she saw was a shy fox that looked over at them and then vanished into the forest. She somehow liked these wonderful new trees. They looked fun to play in. *Should I be scared?* she wondered. *The whole forest is growing fast. Maybe this isn't scary . . . but it sure isn't normal!*

Her hiccupping carried on.

From that time on, nothing was normal anymore in the life of the Knotterfield family. That was something they all realized more every day.

The next morning, Bridget ran to look out. Three more trees had grown in the field: a beech, a maple with strong branches—perfect to build a tree house in—and a spruce. Bridget's hiccups were gone for the moment, but she was not sure whether that would last. When she saw the additional trees, she could not believe her eyes. *They are the perfect hiding place for a wolf, right?*

Nevertheless, she decided it was time to go and see the tree man. Some of her neighbors were standing by the new trees, so she was safe. A few kids were playing around the new trees. They were very young and did not have to go to school yet.

"I want to see if the tree man is still there," Bridget said to Tom.

Be careful," Tom said, but then decided to join her.

"Let's take Towser with us to be sure," Bridget decided.

Towser jumped around happily. *He is not afraid of the wolf coming back,* Bridget thought. They told their mother, who was in the kitchen, where they were going.

"No, get ready for school," she said. "You can see the tree man after school."

"Only for a minute," Bridget begged.

"Okay."

They ran out into the sunshine and found the tree man standing where they built him. But now he was surrounded by firs, staring at a yellow trunk. He was a little crooked but still wore his funny hat.

Towser was barking.

"This is all very strange," Tom said. "When we built him, the field was empty. Now the tree man is completely hidden."

"He is standing in the dark," Bridget said, looking at

the colorful firs.

Soon the neighbors and people in town were discussing the reasons for the rapid tree growth.

"It's from climate change!" some people said.

"No, it's from chemicals in the soil!" said others.

One neighbor, named Douglas Hillerman, thought it was a conspiracy of some environmentalists.

No one knew the true reason until finally, in school, something mysterious happened.

It was only a few weeks before the summer holidays. Bridget's hiccup had been gone again for a few days, and life was normal. Remember, Bridget was not an anxious girl when it came to trees and nature and walking in a dark forest. However, talking in front of her classmates made her very anxious because she was shy.

Her English teacher, Mrs. Petersen, was an older lady with a friendly face and grey hair, always wearing a dress with different kinds of flowers on it. Today, she called Bridget to recite a poem by a famous American called Walt Whitman.

Bridget was excited because the poem had made her very thoughtful. It was all about nature and trees and flowers. But when Mrs. Petersen called her name, Bridget's stomach tightened. Even reciting a wonderful poem made her shyness take over.

"Bridget, give it a try," Mrs. Petersen encouraged.

Bridget stood up, went to the front, and turned around. She stared into twenty-six expectant faces, suddenly feeling the grumble in her stomach. Just when she opened her mouth to share the poem, the hiccup started again.

Hic! Hic!

Some classmates laughed.

"Look, she's shaking." Patty giggled in the first row. She was pretty and cute and always playing everybody's darling. Bridget hated her.

"She is scared," said Lucas, the smart class

representative. They were all giggling and laughing.

"The stage is yours, Miss Knotterfield!" Viv cried from the back. She was tall, with brown, curly hair and a bored face.

Bridget started the poem, gabbling the words so she could get through it fast.

"Slowly," urged Mrs. Petersen.

Bridget blushed. She wanted to continue, but all of a sudden, and before anybody could say anything more, they heard a crack and roar from the schoolyard. It was deafening. Children ran to look out the window.

"It's an earthquake!" shrieked Bridget's best friend, Samantha, a plump blonde girl with green eyes.

"Stay calm," said Mrs. Petersen, looking agitated.

CRRRRRRRRCKK!

Bridget stopped the poem and also went to the window. The noise became louder and louder. She noticed that in the other classrooms windows were opening. In one, Tom looked at her. Soon, dozens of children and their teachers watched the mysterious spectacle outside. Their expressions were confused, excited, marveling, nervous, but mainly . . . *curious.*

The hard tar dissolved in the middle of the schoolyard. Little tar pieces sprayed in the air like a volcanic eruption. The ground rumbled and hissed and, suddenly, the trunk of a tree appeared. It soared upwards, shooting out branches. *Pop, pop, pop*! Colorful leaves exploded open.

"Wow!" someone shouted. "That is a beech tree!"

"It could be an oak tree," cried Lucas.

Bridget saw Tom watching her from the other classroom.

"Kids, that is a maple tree," Mrs. Petersen said calmly. "Look at the leaves."

"I have never seen a tree grow so fast," Samantha said.

It was true. In the middle of the schoolyard stood a wonderful maple tree with a solid trunk and stable branches. It seemed as if this tree had stood there for at least a hundred years.

Curt, a boaster in Tom's class, exclaimed, "This maple tree is perfect for climbing!"

Principal Payne came outside with some colleagues. One of them was his vice principal, Sneyder. They went to the old maple tree that was not old at all. They stopped and stared, with stunned looks.

"Can anybody explain to me how this happened?" Principal Payne shouted.

Nobody could.

"That must have been Bridge," Mandy said with a giggle. She was also a good friend of Bridget's. Her hair was black and short, and she had dark tanned skin like her mother, who was from Mexico. "When she was reciting the poem, she made a *hic*. After that, the tree grew." Mandy was always plainly honest.

The whole class looked at Bridget again. Their faces did not look excited or expectant as before but amused and a bit unsure.

"Nonsense," said Mrs. Petersen.

"Impossible," Lucas agreed.

"That would be freaky," Patty giggled.

But still, they stared at her. Again, Bridget felt uncomfortable. The grumble inside her stomach quickly grew bigger, as fast as the maple tree in the schoolyard. Oh no!

"Me?" she asked, trying to laugh but not sounding very convincing. She wanted to repeat Mrs. Petersen's word but that was interrupted by a gurgling hiccup. "Non—*hic!*—sense!"

Everyone burst out laughing but then went silent again. Listen—*what was that*? There was another cracking noise and Principal Payne's voice shouting, "Oh no, there grows another tree, directly in front of the school entrance!"

CRRRRRRCK!

Again, pieces of tar sprayed, and an oak tree with a blue trunk and yellow leaves grew within minutes and blocked the front entrance.

"How on earth shall we get out of here?" cried Sneyder.

Tom yelled, from the other classroom, "That looks like the oak behind our house!"

I have never seen one with a blue trunk, Bridget thought.

Bridget heard voices calling for help and others shouting, "We are trapped" or "This is weird!"

Sneyder shouted, "We've still got the rear exit. Don't be afraid!"

In the meantime, the oak tree loomed across the front door, its leaves rustling. Bridget stared, entranced by its mighty size. Its leaves licked the air like the tongues of gentle dogs. *Is it possible,* she thought, *that my hiccups are responsible for all this?*

Nonsense! Impossible!

Bridget tried to control the hiccup, but it wouldn't stop. She watched the sun and shadows playing in the oak. It looked like the best tree ever for climbing. Did she dare? Curt scrambled over the windowsill and ran to the glorious maple tree. Principal Payne, Vice Principal Sneyder, and their fellow colleagues were still standing and staring.

"Hey, this is fun!" Curt yelled.

"Stop it!" Sneyder shouted, waking up from his astonishment.

"Come down at once," Principal Payne exhorted.

"Look, nothing bad happens." Curt clapped his hands, and climbed higher.

Laughing and screaming, the children ran into the schoolyard, leaving their teachers speechlessly shaking their heads. Not even Principal Payne or Sneyder could stop the children.

"Can they eat us?" asked a shy little girl.

"No," Tom said, and he grabbed the girl's hand. Together, they climbed the maple tree.

"Do they bite?" a boy asked.

"Can they fly away?" another boy wanted to know.

"No!" shouted Curt from the maple tree. He was already half way up to the top.

"These are all normal trees!" Samantha screamed, climbing the oak. "Only stronger."

"And more colorful!" yelled Lucas.

Curt pointed his nose into the wind. "Smells like a tree," was his comment. It was followed by laughter.

"That is dangerous," cried Payne and looked at Sneyder for help.

"You are not allowed to do that, children!" Sneyder gave it another try. "Come down!"

The children moved like animals in the branches of the two trees. They sang, "Thanks to Bridge, the witch! Thanks to Bridge, the witch!" Teachers appeared in the schoolyard. They talked and discussed and were all muddled up. Nobody knew what to do.

"We need to call the police!"

"No, this is a case for the mayor!"

"First we need to call the fire department!"

"The trees must be cut. They cannot stay there!"

"Oh, that's true. But who will pay for that?"

"That is the responsibility of the Ministry of Natural Resources!"

The happy shouting of the children was deafening.

The Hiccup Girl

Only one child did not join in the whole uproar: Bridget Knotterfield.

With Mrs. Petersen, she stood at the window of her classroom on the first floor of the school house. She stared at her classmates and the other school kids. She saw Tom swinging like Tarzan from a branch. He had a huge grin.

Did I make this epic mess? Bridget wondered. She felt calmer now that nobody was staring at her. *It's nothing but a stupid coincidence*, she thought. *How can a hiccup make a giant tree grow*? But then she saw Mrs. Petersen's troubled gaze and sighed.

After this incident, Bridget's parents were alarmed. Naturally, they did not want to connect their daughter's hiccups with the sudden tree growth. Secretly, however, everybody at school and in the neighborhood did exactly that. People talked in a little town. Word spread dramatically fast if something was happening, especially a phenomenon like the fantasy trees growing all over.

Tom was excited. "You're a tree witch," he said. "Cool!"

Does he mean this? Bridget wondered. *Or is he scared of me?* She felt anxious; it would be terrible if Tom didn't want to build forts in the trees with her anymore or tree men. *Hic, hic, hiccup!*

Her mother took Bridget to two other doctors in another town and then to a specialist in the nearest city. They all agreed it was a normal case of hiccups that would go away.

Confusing.

"Pull your tongue, please. Hold the end of your tongue with your fingers and tug," the first doctor said. "This may sometimes stop hiccups."

Actually, this often does not work, and it did not work for Bridget.

"Sip very cold water slowly," the other doctor said.

Bridget drank.

"Drink a glass of warm water very slowly," the specialist said. "All the way down without breathing."

Bridget held her breath.

The doctors all said, "You just have to wait. And don't worry, they will go away on their own."

But Bridget found it hard not to worry.

Principal Payne decided to have the trees at school cut down. The children protested. They climbed into the branches and surrounded the trees before the men with chainsaws arrived.

"Children, we have to do this," the principal complained. "At the moment, we have to leave through the rear exit because the main entrance is blocked."

"But they are all fantasy trees," the children cried. "No other school has such wonderful trees!"

Even some teachers liked the new, colorful schoolyard. "We need to keep them," Mrs. Petersen said.

Principal Payne shook his head. The men stood around holding their chainsaws. Bridget approached the principal and said, "If it was really me who made these trees grow, I am responsible for them. They need to live."

Vice Principal Sneyder came to help. "I cannot imagine that a small girl like you made this big mess!" he scoffed. "But if it was, you should have taken care that your trees are not blocking the school entry!"

"That's true," Principal Payne replied.

"Please, please, please leave the trees!" Bridget begged.

But no, the principal said that the oak would be cut. However, the maple would stay until after the summer holidays. Principal Payne promised to "think about what to do with it."

I have to come up with a plan to save it, Bridget thought. She was still crying about the death of the oak tree. Now, she would never get to climb it.

The men needed a whole day to cut the oak tree and get the roots out. The trunk, branches, and roots were heavy. Bridget, Samantha, and Mandy stood watching after school. They saw one of the men putting the roots on a truck. He was sweating. The root was big and round and had many smaller secondary roots.

"I need to call my brother," the man said. "He works as a logger and can help me with the roots."

"How come the root is so big?" Samantha asked.

"To keep the tree stable," the man said. "Removing the root is the most difficult work if you cut a tree."

"Did you like the tree?" Bridget wanted to know.

He nodded. "Yes, I am so sorry, little girls. But it blocks the school entrance."

"But it is a fantasy tree," Samantha said. "It has to live. Nobody has such a nice tree on the street."

"I know," the man said. "But I have to cut it. Let's hope your principal will let the maple tree stay where it is. It will be even worse with the roots, to be honest." He laughed.

"What is your name?" Bridget asked, watching him climb into his truck.

"Michael."

The girls did not want to know what he was doing with the cut-off pieces of the oak tree. It was sad enough to see the tree vanishing.

At least the entrance was free again. *Not that I care much about the stupid entrance,* Bridget thought.

The tree was alive and way more cool!

Bridget's neighbors and some of her friends began looking at her very suspiciously. Even Mandy and Samantha sometimes seemed to be watching her doubtfully. However, the three of them were still good friends. They swore on their friendship the day after the trees grew at school.

Bridget carried on going to school and not caring. She had always been popular in her class. Now, she was the big star. Not that she liked that so much, but hey, it was—let's say—okay.

Her classmates were careful about what they said after the latest happenings. The teachers were anxious not to excite her or even frighten her. Wasn't that good? Everybody wanted to please her.

Well . . . *not Principal Payne.*

He thought she should stay home and be sent homework. Her father argued, "There is no proof that Bridget's hiccups caused those trees to grow." Finally, Principal Payne had to let it go but advised his teachers to "be very careful with the girl. We do not want further damage of school premises."

Sometimes Bridget heard people whispering, "If she gets her next hiccup, we need to run—quick!" or "The girl needs to be cured soon." People always need someone to blame.

The truth was, they were all frightened and confused. Nobody knew what to do.

Bridget herself became very sad. How could her beloved trees turn into such a threat?

What if my hiccups didn't stop? She thought. *What if I make more and more trees grow, just so they all have to be killed by chainsaws?*

Hic! Hic!

Bridget ran outside and stared at the waving grass. The tips of new trees broke through the ground, and waved with the grass, then grew taller and pushed out their branches. *Unbelievable!* Bridget thought. *Mega-weird! What can I do?* When, finally, a big oak tree appeared right on the edge of the Knotterfields' back garden, the mood in her family changed. They were all afraid what could happen if this went on, with the trees coming nearer and nearer and growing into the gardens of the houses.

Their neighbors stood by the oak and complained. Mister Hillerman even exclaimed, "Move away!"

Bridget felt even sadder.

The oak tree grew halfway on her parent's property and halfway on the field. *Our garden will soon become a forest,* she thought. *I love forests, but it seems that other people don't.*

Psychologists, doctors and specialists did not have an answer to her hiccup phenomenon. They all said, "Wait, it will disappear."

Tom told some classmates that they could build tree houses in the new oak tree in the garden and tree men in the grass. Word spread and the field filled with children laughing and screaming. Bridget climbed into the oak. Its leaves sang around her and tickled her cheeks. For a little while, she felt perfectly happy. Then it was time to go to her room and do her homework with Samantha. As her feet touched the ground, her anxiety returned.

Samantha saw Bridget was in a bad mood and had an idea.

She suggested, "Let's build a tree house in that oak. We can do homework up there. What do you think?"

"I don't know," Bridged muttered. She loved trees, but she could not understand what was happening.

"It is perfect weather, little witch!" Samantha laughed. "We cannot stay inside, can we?"

"I am not a witch," Bridget claimed.

"But those trees grew after your funny *hic.*"

"That does not mean anything. Besides, it is not funny!"

"They call you the hiccup girl."

Bridget's heart pattered with anxiety. *Is that who I am?* she thought.

A hiccup girl?

The Loggers

"Let's have some fun," Samantha begged. "Come on, I am not interested if it was you or anybody else—I guess it was Mother Nature! Let's go."

Finally, Bridget agreed. They got a ladder and climbed into the oak tree in the garden. Sitting side by side on a broad limb, they enjoyed the wind and sunlight. "Perfect," Bridget said. Samantha climbed down to find wood for a tree house, and Bridget went to get some rope.

Then she had an idea. "Tom and I have an old hammock in the cellar. Let's hang it in the tree."

The "tree house" they finally built turned out to be the huge hammock slung between two branches of the oak. Above it they roped strong limbs from the colored firs as a roof. It looked very cozy.

Bridget and Samantha began having a picnic in the hammock every day. It was a relaxing place and so quiet they could focus on their homework better than ever. Sometimes Mandy joined them. They ate cookies and drank hot chocolate. They were enjoying themselves. No hiccups disturbed them, and no monster wolf cast its shadow.

They liked to watch the kids playing in the trees in the field. Mandy said, "I guess you gave these kids a new kind of playground."

"Thanks," Bridget said. It was wonderful to see that other kids loved trees now too. *But did I really make them grow?* Bridget wondered. *And if I did, who am I?* Worrying about this made her feel odd inside.

"So . . . what are you doing this summer?" Mandy asked.

Bridget said, "I don't know. We have no plans. I guess it will depend on how my hiccups are developing." She sighed. *How could something as simple as hiccups have disrupted my life?* She thought.

"We are going to the ocean," Samantha declared happily. "My parents and I want to go to Vancouver Island."

"I would love to go there," said Bridget. "It has rainforests with huge, tall trees!"

"I am going to Mexico to visit my relatives . . . and to speak more Spanish," Mandy said.

Two days before the end of school, the girls were in the hammock when a big truck stopped beside the field. Bridget had never seen it before. *Ted Wood's Wood Company*, read the lettering on the door panel. A bunch of wild looking guys climbed out and walked to the fantasy trees and started to—*oh no*! They wanted to cut them. They were tree fellers. Their red checkered shirts and blue jeans were dirty with wood shavings and pine sap.

"They want to kill the fantasy trees!" said Mandy.

Bridget cried, "You are right! We need to stop them."

"Calm down," Samantha said, concerned. "You will get another hiccup otherwise."

But Bridget did not care. *I will not let them hurt MY trees*, she thought, balling her fists.

Hastily, she climbed out of the hammock and down the ladder.

"Hold on, wait for us!" Mandy yelled. But Bridget was running as fast as she could go, leaping fallen limbs, crunching over fir cones. A couple of kids were already watching the loggers doing their work. The kids looked upset. No climbing on the fantasy trees anymore; no fantasy playground.

"What are you doing?" Bridget shouted, with angry desperation as the men cleared bushes away from the trees.

One of the men stood a little apart from the others. He seemed to be the leader. He wore a hat, a long muddy coat, and a badge on his chest showing his name, Ted Wood. He looked satisfied.

"What's up?" he asked Bridget.

"Why are you cutting these trees?"

Tom Wood smiled. "Because we were asked to by your community."

Bridget protested, "These are *my* trees!"

"*Your* trees? But they are standing in a field."

"But they do not bother anybody, do they?" Mandy demanded.

"They obviously bother your neighbors and the people in town," said Ted Wood. "They're afraid more trees will go everywhere if we do not cut them down."

"But it was *me* who gave them life!" Bridget started to explain.

Mandy touched her arm. "Ssshhh."

Tom Wood frowned. "What?"

"She made the trees grow in only minutes," one of the kids shouted.

Ted Wood burst out laughing. "That's quite a story! Nice trees, though. So colorful! They will bring a lot of money."

Money?

"But all the kids love these fantasy trees," Samantha said. "Please don't cut them down."

"Don't waste my time, young ladies." He walked over to his men who started their roaring chainsaws.

Helplessly, Bridget watched them cut down the beautiful fantasy trees one after the other. They fell with shrieks and groans and heavy crashes. Then they lay there, like bones in dead bodies. The men sawed them up, put the wood in their truck, and drove away.

Bridget felt terrible. *Why did they have to die?* She thought. *All of us kids loved them!*

"Today is Friday. They will come back on Monday and finish their work," Samantha said.

Mandy sighed. "We need to figure out a plan during the weekend!"

"But what can we do?"

They stared at each other glumly; they did not know.

Bridget didn't really feel like eating dinner that

evening. She pushed her food around on her plate. Her father said, "They are not cutting the whole forest, darling. They're just making sure that no trees are on properties."

"But the ones that were cut were out in the field, not in anyone's yard!" Bridget stated.

"Well, Mayor Richardson decided to finally cut them," her father said with a sigh. He patted Bridget on the shoulder.

"Don't be too upset," her mother said. "Some trees need to be removed."

"We do not know for how long your hiccups will stay," Mr. Knotterfield explained. "If it stays for very long, more and more trees will grow." Bridget gave him an angry look and he added, "Well, I personally like them, but . . . you know how it is."

"We are worried," Mrs. Knotterfield explained, patting Bridget's other shoulder.

"Will they cut the oak tree?" she asked.

"I don't know."

"I mean, it is only standing halfway in the field," Tom explained.

Bridget was desperate. "Dad, do you think that . . . I mean . . . if I do not get my hiccups back, can the oak tree stay?"

"Let's see." Her father sighed again.

But that was the last thing Bridget wanted to do— wait and see. That is what adults always said if they did not know what to do, including her doctors, her teachers, Principal Payne, and now her parents. They always used those words to calm down kids.

She sat silent for the rest of dinner. She was trying to think of a plan to save the fantasy trees, but she could not come up with a solution. Mandy always was the most creative in making plans, so perhaps she would find a solution.

But can I rely on that? Bridget thought. *I am responsible for the trees, so I should think of a plan.*

That evening, Bridget looked out over the field from her bedroom. She missed the colorful firs tossing their boughs. Only a couple of shredded roots stuck out from the soil. Even the tree man she had built with her brother was gone.

Later that evening, Tom knocked at her door. When she opened it, he came and sat on her bed.

"What's up?" she asked.

"How can I get this magic power you have—I mean, to grow trees?"

"You know where it came from!"

Tom sighed. "Yes, but . . . I want to have it too. So do I need to go out at night and see the monster wolf?"

"It is not so easy, Tom, having this power. It scares me. Only God should have the power to give life, to people and to nature."

"I guess, but it would be great at school, wouldn't it? You are a star now. Bridge, the witch!"

"I hate that expression." She looked at Tom, a six-year-old not feeling happy in his class. *He is still so small*, she thought. His classmates are teasing him, and his best friend is Curt, the phony. Sure it would be great if he had magic power to grow trees. Truth was she felt bad for him. "And I hate it when they say I am the hiccup girl. If you grow trees, we'll be the hiccup *family*."

"Not good," Tom admitted.

"A tree only grows when I am scared, remember? Why would you want to be scared, Tom?"

He shrugged and scuffed his toes on the rug. Then he stood to leave the room but stopped at the door. "We can ask the mayor."

"What do you mean?"

"Just an idea if we want to save the fantasy trees."

Save the Fantasy Trees

"We need to talk to the mayor," Mandy said when they sat under the maple tree in the schoolyard the next morning. The sun was shining and only a few days were left before the summer holidays.

Bridget was tired. She'd barely slept, thinking about how they could persuade the neighbors and the people in town to save the fantasy trees. "How do you want to do that?" she asked.

"My dad works at the mayor's office. I will speak to him this evening!"

"I don't think he will just change his mind because some girls are begging him not to cut down the fantasy trees," Samantha said doubtfully.

Tom and Curt wandered over and sat down.

"I have an idea!" Bridget explained and shared it with her friends.

"Could work," Mandy finally said.

"Let's try!" Samantha agreed as the bell rang for classes to begin.

Bridget had to gather all her courage to overcome her shyness and share her plan with everyone in her class. She had to speak loud and clear even though her voice wanted to be a whisper. Tom and Curt would do the same in their classes. During the break they wanted to get other kids to adopt their plan.

Bridget took a deep breath and glanced at the wall

clock. Mrs. Petersen would arrive at any minute. Bridget stood as tall and straight as she could. "We want to collect signatures on a petition," she explained. "We'll ask for the fantasy trees stay where they are. We want all your parents to sign on a list we present to the mayor."

"But Bridge, you can easily perform your magic and create some new fantasy trees," Patty said.

"No. Well, that is not so easy."

"You need to be scared?"

"Excited?" Lucas asked. "Terrified?"

Some others shouted, "You are Bridge, the witch! Make your magic."

"You are the hiccup girl!"

Bridget blushed red. *I hate being the center of attention,* she thought.

"Look we really need your help," Mandy said. "We all know that Bridge does not like her hiccups and hopes it will be gone soon."

Bridget nodded. "Yes, and the only thing that is left then is a bunch of fantasy trees."

"We do not want to lose them," Samantha begged. "So please help us, at least in favor of the fantasy maple tree in the schoolyard."

Mrs. Peterson opened the door and obviously only heard the last word.

"What is going on here?" she asked, looking concerned. She glanced at Bridget and seemed relieved. Everything was okay. No hiccups.

"We want you to sign a list against the cutting of the trees." Mandy presented the paper to the teacher.

"That certainly includes the maple tree in the schoolyard," Bridget quickly added.

Mrs. Petersen was now concerned in another way. "What are you kids up to?"

"We want to save the fantasy trees." Samantha smiled, always optimistic.

The teacher shook her head. "Well . . . I don't know."

Lucas finally helped them. "Bridge has created the trees and I think, well . . . she should decide whether they stay or not."

"But there will be more of those trees if she hiccups again!" Patty snapped. She stopped when she saw Bridget's face, now red with fury. "Well, perhaps you are right, they are beautiful and . . . unique!"

Mrs. Peterson sighed, but finally she signed the petition.

It was their first signature.

During the breaks, they convinced a lot of other kids to ask their parents to sign the petition. They also asked the teachers and Principal Payne, but he did not sign nor did Sneyder.

"Let's see," they said. "The decision about what happens with the maple tree in the schoolyard is our decision, *not* the mayor's!"

After school, Samantha, Mandy, and Bridget hurried back to the Knotterfields' house. Tom was joining them with Curt and Lucas. They decided to go down the streets of their neighborhood and ask people to sign.

That was not an easy task as many of the neighbors were against the fantasy trees. Well, most of them were not really against them; they only feared there would be more and more of them, spreading over from the field and into their nice gardens.

But some of the neighbors signed the list.

Mr. and Mrs. Grady, for example. They were living opposite of the Knotterfields´ house, and they'd known Tom and Bridget since they were born. They did not expect the fantasy trees to get closer to *their* garden. There were other houses in front of theirs, so the trees could not really bother them.

Gilbert and Lucy Franklin signed as well. They lived next to the Knotterfields´ and had twin babies, Mac and Tony, who were just one year old. Yes, they were frightened of the fantasy trees, but they loved nature too and "Hmmm, eventually there is a way to stop the trees from growing," Mr. Franklin said. Bridget liked him.

Clearly, Mr. Hillerman did not sign the list. He was one of the most suspicious people Bridget had ever met. He had conspiracy theories about everything. Certainly, he knew the rumor that was going on in town: This little girl Bridget Knotterfield had magic power. He did not even let them in when they knocked at his door. "You are a witch," he snapped.

Normally Bridget would have been very sad about such a comment, but this time she was not. She was angry! It made her even more determined to persuade people that the "magic" she did was good. The fantasy trees were not a danger.

However, it was similar with Mrs. Spencer who lived a couple of houses up the street. She was against everything that was going on in the town. She was always grumpy and did not like children at all. As a result, she was happy not to sign their list. Bridget was convinced she was very lonely and did not even hear the rumor about her.

When they came out of Mrs. Spencer's house, Bridget saw her father, Tom, Curt, and Lucas standing in front of the Knotterfields' house.

"What are you doing?" Her father asked, angrily.

"We are trying to save the fantasy trees," said Bridget, but her father stalked off indoors.

Later, her parents sat silent at dinner. Mr. Knotterfield grunted, eating his vegetable soup.

"We will present this list to Mayor Richardson, and he will stop the men from cutting trees," Bridget explained.

"Hmmm," her mother sighed.

"Cool idea," Tom said.

Bridget's father looked over at his wife for help, but she shook her head. "The people in town are frightened of what happened," he said.

Tom giggled. "I am not frightened of some great trees. And Bridge isn't either. Look, she did not get a hiccup in the last few days."

"Maybe it is over," Bridget said hopefully. "Those trees should stay. There is no town around that has such nice trees."

"That's true," Mr. Knotterfield admitted, scrolling over the list of people who'd signed. There were many signatures. "How many do you need?"

"A hundred. That is what Mandy said. She knows from her dad. He works at the mayor's office."

"So far, we've got ninety-four," Tom said.

"Please," Bridget begged.

He father was still thinking, but her mother grabbed a pen and took the list. "Now you've got ninety-five.

Let's see where we get to with this!"

Maybe Mr. Knotterfield felt the pressure. His face looked concerned when he took the pen from his wife.

"Hope you will get to a hundred."

"We've got ninety-nine signatures," Mandy said when the girls met the next day. It was Sunday. They sat in the hammock tree house in the fantasy oak tree in the Knotterfields' garden, swinging back and forth. The last three signatures had come from Michael, the man who helped cut the oak tree in the schoolyard, and Mandy's parents who'd finally agreed on signing.

"So, we still need one final signature," Samantha moaned.

"Let's go to the mayor anyway," Bridget urged. "Let's give it a try!"

"Dad's having Sunday lunch with Mayor Richardson

today at noon," Mandy said. "It is at Winnie's Tea Room in town."

Samantha looked at her watch. "Then we've only got half an hour."

Winnie's Tea Room was a restaurant popular for its good food and various sorts of tea and coffee. Mayor Richardson loved the cakes there.

The girls took the bus to the town center and arrived at Winnie's a bit after noon. It was full and noisy. The girls stared around at the old-style, antique furniture. The tables were laid with ruffled cloths, and the dishes looked like they were from the last century. Waiters in a black-and-white uniforms hurried around, and the air was filled with the noise of dozens of people.

"There he is." Mandy pointed to a man eating cheesecake with a lot of cream. He was a chubby man in his mid-forties with a mustache and a satisfied grin. He wore casual pants, a shirt, and a bow tie and was talking to another man, Mandy's father.

The girls slipped into the crowded room. Bridget

had been here a couple of times before with Tom and her parents but never had she felt so nervous. She wiped her sweaty palms on her jeans. *Please be quiet, stomach,* she thought. *Everything's good. We are saving the trees.* But her stomach grumbled. *No hiccups now!* She pleaded. *That will destroy our whole mission. Please!*

"Dad!" Mandy shouted and waved. Her father knew they were coming to give Mayor Richardson the signatures list, but he pretended not to know. Bridget noticed a bead of sweat on his forehead.

"Mayor Richardson, we need to talk to you," Samantha squeaked.

Bridget gulped, opened and closed her mouth. No hiccups. *Be brave,* she told herself. "We just need a couple of minutes of your time, please," she told the mayor.

Mayor Richardson looked up, worried about the interruption. He had a cream-spotted napkin around his neck. „Well, what is it?" he asked gruffly.

"We want you to leave the fantasy trees where they

are," Mandy continued. Mayor Richardson frowned in a moment of confusion.

"The ones in the grassy field." Samantha helped his memory.

"And the maple tree in our schoolyard," Bridget added. "We . . . we have a list with signatures against the cutting of the trees."

"Fantasy trees? Ah, you mean the colored firs."

"They are gone already, but we want to save the other ones," Bridget explained. She wiped her sweaty palms on her legs again.

Fighting down the grumble inside her, she put the list of signatures in front of the mayor. He took it hesitantly, glancing at his cheesecake, and read out loud:

'Dear Mayor Richardson . . . hmmm . . . We, the people of this town, declare that we do not accept the cutting of the trees in the field. They do not bother us and should stay. Please revise your order to cut them immediately.'

The mayor scrolled down the pages with all the signatures, read some names out loud, and frowned.

"You signed, too, Albert?" he asked Mandy's father.

"Yes, I . . . well, I think we should have asked more people before making the decision to cut these colorful trees. Not everyone is frightened of them."

"*Wrong*! Most of them are! At least the neighbors of—" He took a closer look at Bridget. It seemed as if he'd just realized who she was. "You are the girl that caused all this, right?" he whispered.

"That is not proven," Samantha quickly replied.

Bridget gasped and turned red again. The grumble in her stomach became worse. *Oh no*! "I don't really know," she whispered.

"It is not proven," Mandy repeated while Mayor Richardson watched Bridget, rattling his fork against his cheesecake plate.

Mandy's father said, "These kids have worked really hard to collect all the signatures about the fantasy trees and—"

Hic!

Everyone stared at Bridget. She wished she could curl up into a small ball and disappear. "Was that her famous hiccup that causes the trees?" the mayor asked, sounding amused.

Hic!

He did not need any further explanation. A long roaring came from the patio outside the tea room. People looked around in sudden confusion. Their conversations stopped and everybody peered outside through the high windows. Beside the terrace was a small garden with grass. The roaring rose to a rumble and a cracking. A tree trunk appeared in the grass, flinging mud across the patio.

CRRRRRRCK!

Within seconds, a wonderful red fir was growing from the ground, towering upwards, shooting out boughs, then fragrant needles and growing thick bark.

Expelled

The mayor sat with his mouth hanging open. So did Mandy's father and the people in Winnie's.

Only Samantha was laughing. "The Christmas trees are back!" she cried.

"At least one of them," Mandy mumbled.

Bridget heard somebody saying, "Is that a redwood or a fir?"

Mayor Richardson did not finish his meal; instead, he ordered what he called a "calm-downer." The truth was he had not believed the people until he saw it with his own eyes. Bridget Knotterfield was nervous, excited, and frightened. And her hiccup had created another fir.

Winnie appeared with some of his waiters, looking into the garden. Bridget was expecting a furious cry, but it did not come. A few of his guests crept out from under the tables.

"That is exactly what we needed," one of the waiters said. "Some shade for the patio."

"That colorful tree is very decorative," another waiter said.

Mandy gave her friends a short sign: Let's get out of here. "Nothing happened, ladies and gentlemen," she cried, thumbs up. "Nobody got hurt—all okay."

Then they rushed out, passing Winnie who was unsure whether he should be happy about the new tree in his garden or not.

The next day was Monday, and the tree cutters came back.

Bridget was alone in her hammock tree house in the garden. That morning, her mother had a call from Principal Payne. Bridget had stood beside her, listening to the conversation on speaker phone. Once again the principal was frightened, and wanted to keep Bridget out of school. *Everybody* in town knew about her hiccup at Winnie's. *Everybody* was sure that it was her nervous hiccups that caused the growing of the new fantasy Christmas tree—and all the other trees. Principal Payne's opinion was that *everybody* in school would look at Bridget—which she did not like—and that would eventually cause another hiccup, which would cause new trees to grow, which would cause fresh anger and so on.

"But she needs to go to school," her mother had said strictly. "You cannot just let her stay away!"

"Just for the last two days before the summer holidays begin," Principal Payne answered.

So now Bridget sat alone in the oak tree, feeling sad and missing her friends at school. It wasn't fair!

Become a brave girl, she thought, *and then the hiccup will not come again, will it? I mustn't let my fears take control.* But Bridget knew this was easier thought than done. Her first test was about to arrive with the tree fellers.

She saw the truck arriving near the field. She had brought some binoculars and watched Ted Wood and his bunch stomp up the path through the field towards her parents´ house. One of his men was carrying a chainsaw. It seemed they'd come to cut down the oak tree she was sitting in.

When they stood beneath it, she climbed on a strong branch. "Stop!" she shouted.

Ted Wood frowned then sighed. "My young lady again, the holy ghost of the trees. Can I ask you to come down, please?"

"This tree is not completely in the field," Bridget replied. "It must stay."

"Oh, I am not so sure," Ted said, pretending to measure the exact location of the tree with a measuring stick. "I guess it is two-thirds in the field."

His men snickered. Then one of them made a terrible mistake. He started his chainsaw. Its roaring whine filled Bridget's whole head.

She gulped nervously. It was not only the noise, but also the man's scowl and swagger that scared her. Only one thing was clear; this man would cut her tree, not caring if she was still in it. *Hic.*

She felt the grumble in her stomach coming. Then she saw her father heading towards her. At the same time, she heard a humming—and it was not coming from the chainsaw.

"What is going on here?" her father asked in alarm. "Bridget, come down please."

"It is in the field!" Ted Wood yelled.

Mr. Knotterfield said quietly, "Let's not get excited. It is *our* tree, gentlemen. I planted it some years ago."

Ted looked skeptical. He obviously did not believe a word. But he did not have time to think about it.

A humming from the grass grew into a loud CRRRRRRCK!

A couple of roots from the firs that had been cut began to grow into a new tree. It was another red fir, and its branches were very dense. It was a perfect Christmas tree, similar to the one at Winnie's Tea Room. However, it kept growing until it was the tallest fir in the forest.

"That is fantastic!" Ted Wood shrieked.

"That is worth a fortune!" another man shouted. "Was that you, young lady?

Her father answered before Bridget could say a word. "That is Mother Nature. Nobody except her has the power to make trees grow."

Nobody except her and Bridget Knotterfield.

Suddenly a car bumped up the path and stopped beside them. Mandy's father, Mr. Bradley, got out. "I have a decision on the tree cutting from Mayor Richardson," he said. "The trees will stay!"

Bridget could not believe her ears. She hugged herself happily.

"What do you mean with the trees will stay?" Ted Wood wanted to know.

"It means your work is done, sir. You get paid and then you can go."

Ted looked confused and signaled his men to stop their chain saws. "That means we are *not allowed* to cut them anymore."

"Exactly," Mr. Bradley agreed. "The kids collected one hundred signatures from people against the tree cutting. Our mayor has to respect that!"

Bridget scrambled down the oak, her binoculars still in her hand. She was amazed. "But we only got ninety-nine signatures!"

"We got one more!"

"Whose?" her father asked.

"Winnie signed when he decided to keep the nice, uh, red Christmas tree on his terrace." He paused. "I need to add that there is a condition. There will be no additional trees in this park."

"That condition is broken already," Ted snapped. "She just created that red fir over there."

Mr. Bradley pretended to be surprised when he saw the new tree. He seemed to like it, though. "This happened before I came." He smiled but gave Bridget a warning wink.

Bridget was thrilled! Victory! *Now, I need to get cured of the hiccups as soon as possible. No new tree is allowed to grow in the field.*

But to find a cure had so far proved impossible.

"I need to tell my friends!" she said, dancing with joy. She rushed to school and shared the great news with her class. She didn't notice Principal Payne standing outside, listening.

"In this school I, not the mayor, make decisions," he muttered to himself.

Starting the Journey

In the evening, the Knotterfields sat to make final plans about their summer. They had to stick together now and keep the promise they gave to Mayor Richardson: No new tree in the field meant that Bridget had to get rid of her hiccups, right? But *how*? And *where*?

Her father had already made the decision for them all. "We are going to visit Aunt Claire," he said.

Mrs. Knotterfield's sister lived on an apple farm

near a small town up north. It was not often that they visited her because the journey took two days. Normally, Aunt Claire came to visit them, usually at Christmas or Thanksgiving.

"*Ugh*!" said Tom with a sigh.

"I don't want to stay at a lonely place like Aunt Claire's for the whole summer break. Thanks, Bridge!"

"I like the idea," Bridget replied. She loved the apple trees and the forest behind Aunt Claire's house. Towser agreed with a bark. For him the forest was a paradise.

The last day of school arrived. Bridget's mother called Principal Payne and promised, "Bridget will be cured from her hiccups when we come back."

Mr. Knotterfield prepared the RV. Inside it was a tiny kitchen, a little sitting corner, and four beds in two rows. The top was for Bridget and her brother, the lower compartment for their parents.

As soon as the school day ended, the family was

on the highway heading north. Two days of driving were in front of them. Bridget looked out of the window. She wished they were arriving at her aunt's much sooner; she wanted to relax and figure out how to get rid of her hiccups.

Tom was playing a game on his phone. He had not said a word since they started. But then he put his phone away and stared out the window.

"What's wrong, little man?" Mr. Knotterfield asked, watching his son in the rearview mirror.

"I get teased at school," Tom complained. "It's because of Bridge and her magic power."

"Bridge does not have magic power," Mrs. Knotterfield said.

"Everybody in class thinks it's cool. A girl with magic power! But I don't have any power! I am only the little brother of a witch girl." Tom scowled. "How can I get the power? I mean—just for a while."

"I don't want to hear you talk like this," said their father. "Bridge will recover again."

"Yes, I will," Bridget insisted.

"We will all have a good time at Aunt Claire's farm," mother said. "We will stay at her house until Bridge's hiccups are over."

Bridget could see in her mother's eyes that her hope was bigger than her confidence.

The next hours they drove straight on. Not many cars were on the road. They passed little villages and towns and sometimes farmhouses. But these became fewer and were replaced by forests. They drove into loneliness.

Bridget thought, *There are so many trees around, it doesn't matter if I make more grow. I am already far away from the danger zone. Far away from my friends and classmates and neighbors and people who talk about me and my terrible hiccups.*

She smiled. She felt relaxed now. Her hiccups were far away. The whole world was far away. She fell asleep and woke up when Towser licked her ear.

Finally, when evening came, her father stopped the RV at an empty campsite and opened a map, studying it to be ready for the next day.

"Let's collect wood for a nice campfire." mother smiled. She loved campfires. She was very old style when it came to romantic scenarios with the whole family.

"Is there a lake somewhere?" Tom asked.

"I am afraid not."

Tom murmured something like "boring" but followed his family reluctantly to get the fire started. Later, as they sat around the fire eating dinner, Tom gave Bridget a scowling glance from time to time. He and Bridget rarely fought. *This will be the most boring summer ever,* his eyes seemed to say.

Bridget was completely relaxed in bed in the RV that night. As long as she was not anxious or excited, everything was good. Would the hiccups really vanish in the days to come?

She thought, *Maybe the air is different at Aunt*

Claire's farmhouse. But what if I see the monster wolf again? We are heading up north. Maybe the wolf is still out there.

She stroked Towser's head. He slept next to her, breathing steadily. A million times now, Bridget had asked herself how she could have been so curious and walked out into the darkness to see what was happening near the tree man. How could she have done that? It was dangerous, even without a monster wolf.

During the night, she woke up and heard owls hooting. Towser was now lying at her feet. She opened a window and listened to the wind rustling through the trees. She loved that sound; she'd grown up with it. The trees in the forest behind her parents' house always rustled. And so too did the fantasy trees since growing a few weeks ago.

Since then her whole life had changed. She'd never thought of trees being threatening. *What an odd thought!*

She could not sleep and finally stood up. Silently she

tiptoed through the RV to the door. Towser raised his head and watched her. Her parents were sleeping below her compartment. So was Tom. They were all lying in a big bed. She giggled. Sometimes, but very seldom lately, Tom crawled into their parents´ bed during the night. She could hear them all breathing or snoring.

Nobody had noticed her sneaking around. She pushed the door open and took a deep breath. A fresh wind blew in her face. The mountains were not far away.

There was a small fear that the monster wolf was somewhere around, so she sat on the steps of the RV, ready to jump inside if it appeared. Towser was right behind her, resting his head on her shoulder. She sat listening—breathing the air of the trees. No fantasy trees were around.

Nothing happened. No hiccups and no cracking noise of growing trees. Towser was sniffing beside her. She held his collar.

Was that a wolf howling? No—Towser's sniffing

was not a sign that there was a danger. The moonlight created shadows under a group of black poplars. However, the air smelled of spruces and oaks and maples.

The next moment, she was asleep.

Her father's voice woke her. "Bridge, what are you doing there?"

It was still dark. Bridget was tired and feeling uncomfortable, slouched against the doorframe. Towser was lying next to her. She was shivering. "I'm sorry. I just wanted fresh air and . . ."

"Come back in," her father said, yawning.

Bridget stood up slowly and sneezed. *Hatscheeeeee!*

A couple of minutes later she was asleep in her bed.

They had breakfast again at the fireplace and drove without another break until lunchtime. "We only have a short break today," Mr. Knotterfield explained. "We will be at Aunt Claire's at dinner time."

"I am not so hungry," Bridget said.

"Why does Aunt Claire live so far away?" Tom moaned.

"She left the stinky city for the loneliness of the farmland and the apple trees," mother said. "It made her happier."

Their father nodded. "Her husband bought this farm long ago."

"But he is dead now, isn't he?" Bridget asked.

"That's true." Her mother sighed.

Aunt Claire's husband had died three years ago. Since then, she had managed the apple farm alone, which meant more hard work for her. She had some hired help though. Since Winston's death, his co-worker, Henry, helped Aunt Claire in her daily business. He was the foreman, and he always had a smile on his face and seemed happy. Bridget had loved him on her last trip north. *Maybe he will know how to get over my fears and my hiccups,* she thought.

A Tree Man in the Field

At lunchtime, they stopped where the highway crossed a small river. A little bridge led across it. Nearby was open ground, a perfect parking space. It was next to a field of barley. It was Bridget who first spotted the field and asked them to stop there. They all went outside and enjoyed the noise of barley rustling in the wind. What a wonderful place!

"Let's go for a walk along the river," father suggested.

Mother said, "I will stay here and prepare lunch, some cookies and tea and stuff."

Mr. Knotterfield walked to the river with Tom and Bridget, with Towser following. They strolled along the banks and enjoyed the crystal-clear water. The field of barley next to them smelled fresh and continued on the other side of the river. Towser vanished into the field, and a little later they heard him barking and yapping.

"Let's go play hide and seek," Bridget suggested and jumped into the field of barley. The others chased behind but soon could not find her anymore.

Before long, they were all lost.

"Where are you, Bridge?" she heard her father shout.

"I am here!"

"*Where?*"

"I cannot see Towser," Tom said. A short yapping was the answer. Bridget was happy running through the field. Stalks of barley tickled her. She happened to see Tom's shadow some distance away. At least she thought it was his. "I will find you, Tom," she sang. Her brother did not reply. Instead, the shadow quickly moved away and vanished.

The barley became denser, and after a while, she could not see very far. She jumped to spot Tom. She saw her father at the end of the field, near the river.

"Got you, Tom!" he shouted proudly and lifted his son above the stalks. They were both laughing.

The shadow Bridget had seen before obviously wasn't Tom's.

"We need to catch Bridge," she heard Tom saying. "Where is she, Towser? Let's find her."

The dog was barking.

"I am here!" she yelled. "I win the game!" She carried on.

But hold on—*what was that?*

She heard a noise that sounded very familiar. It was an unpleasant sound that rang inside her ears. She scrunched up her face. She knew that it came from a chainsaw and remembered all the cut trees in her hometown. She jumped and looked around. Beyond the field, she saw woodland—and birds escaping from the noise.

They were cutting trees somewhere.

She moved on. But she did not get very far. Suddenly, she came to a small space in the middle of the barley. It was just big enough for a single person to stand in without being tickled by the stalks. Somebody was indeed standing there and when Bridget reached the place, the person seemed to move.

Then she realized who-—or better—what it was. It was a tree man, similar to the one Tom and she had built behind their home. But this one was much more frightening! It had long straight arms made of branches. They were stiff and looked like a cross above the scary head carved from a root. The head was wiggling. There was no smile, no mouth at all. There were only eyes that were little holes. The tree man wore red dungarees, a yellow shirt, and a straw hat.

Bridget was chilled with terror. A tree man couldn't move, could it? Or was it a scarecrow? She forgot about the noise of the chainsaw and watched the tree man moving away quickly as soon as he noticed her. The thing vanished, snickering, behind the stalks.

Bridget ran as fast as she could. *What is going on here? Who is that strange figure?* She thought. Soon Towser came barking, happy that he'd found her. She ran straight past him.

Then she heard her father's voice. "Got you, Bridge! Let's meet back at the river."

When she reached the bank, Tom and her father were waiting. They were all covered with barley. It looked funny, but . . . Bridget was frightened. Her father realized at once that something was wrong. "You okay?" he asked.

"There is a tree man in the field," she gasped. "But it moved away."

Her father stared with a puzzled frown.

"Tree man cannot move," Tom said.

"This one can!"

"But then it was human and not a tree man," her father said.

"It was not human, I am sure!"

She again felt the grumble in her stomach. *Please*, she thought, *not a hiccup. Not now!* Then, suddenly, something hard hit the back of her head.

"*Ouch!*"

Mr. Knotterfield turned around, shocked. His movement towards his kids saved him. Something hard flew in his direction from the barley and only just missed him.

The next moment, Tom cried, "*Ouch*—I am hit!"

Their father shouted "*Down!*" and they knelt. A little stone was lying by the river. He carefully reached for it and looked at it incredulously. "Who on earth is throwing stones at us?" he asked. The next moment he was hit by another one.

"*Ouch!*" he shrieked and grabbed his head.

They heard someone snickering in the field. It was the same sound Bridget had heard from the tree man before. It sounded like a kid that had played a trick on somebody. Another stone flew over them and splashed into the river.

"*Hide!*" Mr. Knotterfield screamed, and they jumped behind some stalks of barley.

Wonderful Palm Trees

Bridget looked in the direction where the stone had disappeared into the water. She recognized the strange tree man standing on the other side of the river. Behind him was another field. He was waving at her, his head wiggling. How did this thing get across the river so quickly?

"There he—*hic!*—is," she whispered. The tree man again vanished within a second, but at least her father must have seen it this time.

"What the heck is that?" Mr. Knotterfield asked. They heard the snickering again and then—silence!

The tree man had vanished into the field on the other side. Towser barked angrily in that direction.

"My head hurts," Tom cried tearfully.

Their father took a cloth out of his pocket and went carefully over to the river to make it wet. "Put that on your forehead," he said. "Bridge?"

"I am okay." She felt to see if her head was bleeding, but it wasn't, only pounding.

"Let's get back to the RV," he said. "Quick!"

But it was too late.

Bridget's body was shaken by another big *hic*! They all stood still for a moment, dazed and not moving. Instead, they were waiting. A dull cracking was heard and then a rumble. The ground at the river dissolved and little pieces of mud and sand sprayed in the air. The trunk of a tree appeared and quickly grew bigger and bigger. And bigger. It formed branches with huge green leaves.

"That's a palm tree," Tom said, confused.

Mr. Knotterfield watched the tree growing and shook his head. He'd never believed in magic, but maybe he should, especially these days. "Look at this, done by my daughter," he muttered to himself, sounding like he was in a trance. "Yes, she loves trees, and now she is even able to grow them out of nowhere. That's *magic* indeed!"

He looked scared.

Suddenly Bridget heard her mother`s voice. "Where are you?" she cried, sounding worried.

"We are here!" her father answered. "Be careful." Then he saw another stone flying in her direction. "Watch out!" he shouted and—as a reflex—her mother ducked. The stone missed her.

"What is going on here?" she asked, terrified.

"The tree men are attacking us with stones!" Tom shouted. "And Bridge has another hiccup."

"What?" Mrs. Knotterfield looked at the palm tree. "Where did that come from?"

"Bridge!"

"We will explain later," father urged. "Let's get back to the RV first."

Silently, they walked back, alongside the barley. Mr. Knotterfield put a finger to his lips and said, "Shhh." He stood up and peeked over the stalks. He moved his head back and forth, and then came down again.

"I cannot see anything. They must be gone."

They met Mrs. Knotterfield under the palm tree, and the whole family silently crawled over to where they had parked the RV. Bridget's mother had put some camping chairs and a table outside. It would have been a wonderful lunch, but now it was too dangerous to eat there. They climbed inside and hastily Tom and Bridget told their mother what had happened in the field.

"How did you decide to grow a palm tree?" mother asked.

"It was not *me!*" Bridget replied, angrily. "I can't decide what grows!" She tried to listen to her body. It felt calm again. They were safe inside. Nothing more could happen, could it?

"Let's move on," mother decided and moved towards the front seat. "Sit down, kids."

But Bridget did not sit down.

Her eyes were still focused on the field. "There it is again!" she shrieked and pointed towards the field. In the middle of it stood the tree man with the red pants, the yellow shirt, and the straw hat. He was waving at them again, wiggling his head.

They all gasped in shock.

It looked weird as the wooden branches moved, like a skeleton's bones. Towser started to bark while Bridget took a deep breath. *Don't let me hic,* she pleaded, *no hiccups, please. I am far away from this . . . beastly creature.*

Then the tree man was gone.

Breakdown

Now Mr. Knotterfield was furious. "That's enough! I will check this out."

"Let's go," Mrs. Knotterfield said. "It's only kids playing tricks."

But Bridget's father rushed outside, grabbed a big stick lying on the ground, and ran into the field.

"Stay in the RV!" he shouted. "I will be right back. Don't worry, Bridge, all is good. Towser will come with me."

The dog and her father vanished into the field. Bridget was gasping. Again, she felt the grumble in her stomach. She leaned out the open door and took deep breaths of fresh air and the sweet scent of the barley. Her mother stood next to her, but Tom preferred looking out a closed window. "I do not want to be hit again by a stone," he said. They saw some stalks moving and guessed it was their father. The tree man was not to be seen.

"Come back!" Mrs. Knotterfield shouted, anxiously.

Bridget was fighting against the grumble in her stomach when suddenly a short, but threatening, *hic!* escaped.

"There it starts again." Tom sighed, holding the cloth against his forehead.

The noises of the world seemed to stop for a moment; no birds sang, no crickets chirped, and the rustling was still. The next moment, they heard the

CRRRKKKK of growing trees. It came from the place they had been before, right by the river. Next to the palm tree grew—literally within a minute—a second palm tree with huge green leaves, even bigger than the first one.

"Now I got my beach! Thanks, Bridge," Tom joked.

Mrs. Knotterfield's face turned pale. "What on *earth* shall we do? I thought our trip to Aunt Claire's would help get rid of this terrible hiccup. Now it's getting worse, just because of some kids playing tricks."

Towser gave a short bark and then he and Mr. Knotterfield came out of the field. The wooden stick was still in his hand.

"Did you see him, Dad?" Tom and Bridget asked.

"Nothing," their father gasped, bending over to catch his breath. Straightening up, he barked, "We've got a flat tire!"

Bridget carefully looked outside. When she saw the sagging tire, her anxiety got worse again.

"Be careful of the stones!" Tom shouted.

"I will call the tow truck," mother said and grabbed her mobile.

"I already tried it," Bridget gasped. "No reception."

"What the—" Mrs. Knotterfield stopped herself.

Calm down. All is good, thought Bridget. There is no tree man anywhere. She checked the field on the other side of the river but could not see anybody. *I am frightened of a tree man? I have built so many of them, with branches and roots and cord, and now I am running away from them? It was just a kid's joke,* she repeated to herself. *A kid's joke. A kid's joke!*

"If we can't get a tow truck, we'll just have to drive on the flat until we reach a garage," father said grimly. "Let's hope we don't destroy the rim." He climbed inside and started the engine.

"Here we go!" But it did not start.

It made a rattling noise, then a short sputtering growl, and died. Mr. Knotterfield tried again with the same result. *RATATATATATAAAT*.

A third and fourth try were unsuccessful. He got out and opened the hood, carefully looking around. "This is getting strange," he mumbled. He gave the RV an angry kick. His family joined him and looked into the engine.

"Somebody cut some cables," Bridget noticed.

"Yes," her father agreed. "It's the cable going to the alternator."

"Somebody obviously does not want us to meet Aunt Claire," Tom said.

Bridget looked over to the two palm trees standing in the sunlight. And then she saw the tree man again. It was waving from the other side and then vanished into the field.

"The tree man!" she shouted.

"Somebody wants to frighten us," Tom said and rushed back inside. Again, Bridget had to fight against the terrible feeling in her stomach.

"Don't be scared, kids," their father tried to calm them down. "I am sure that was an animal that bit the cables."

"The monster wolf," Bridget assumed.

"Let's go back home," Tom moaned.

"The tree men are following us," Bridget whispered. *Hic, hic!*

The earth suddenly grumbled. The whole RV was shaking.

"An earthquake!" shouted Tom from inside, sounding terrified. "Bridge has caused an earthquake!"

The ground next to the van swelled up and pieces of mud erupted. A trunk appeared and grew bigger and bigger. Its branches were small, but the leaves were massive.

Mr. Knotterfield shouted and ran towards the RV and jumped in to be with Tom. Bridget and her mother threw themselves flat on the ground. A loud bang made them jump with fright. The RV toppled over on its side.

CRRRRRRCK.

Then there was silence.

The RV's windows and the door were on top, and so were two of the four wheels and one of the front seats. Next to the chassis, another palm tree was standing, bigger and stronger than the other two with huge leaves in yellow, red, blue, and purple.

Bridget was frozen and stared desperately at the high palm. *"What have I done?"* she cried. Tears flowed down her cheeks.

Her mother grabbed her and tried to comfort her. "It's not your fault."

"It is. Please, I want it to stop! I cannot stand this anymore!"

The door opened on the top, and Mr. Knotterfield climbed out. "Give me your hand, Tom," he said.

"My head hurts," Tom said. "That is all Bridge's fault!"

Bridget only cried. She could not say a word. She was not sure whether she still liked trees or not. She liked the fantasy trees—yes! They looked fantastic and they were created only by her, Bridget Knotterfield. On the other hand, she could not do anything about this weird hiccupping. Even if she wanted to stop the whole magic tree growing, she could not. It was overwhelming.

Suddenly she heard the voice of her brother. "Bridge

must go away!" he said, crying. He was bleeding from another cut. Father put another piece of cloth on it. "Bridge must go away!"

The family sat there, not knowing what to do.

The pain inside Bridget was terrible. She had endangered her whole family. Their whole trip was at risk. Tom was right; she needed to go. But *where*? Go home alone? Take a train?

"I have to take Tom to a doctor," her father said, standing up and holding his map. "There is a little town two and a half miles from here. I will speak to the police and try to find a garage." Then he went to the river and dipped the cloth in the water. When he came back, Tom whined, "I want to go home!"

"We can't do that with a broken-down RV," Mr. Knotterfield sighed. "Let's stick to our plans. It won't be better at home . . . with Bridget having this terrible hiccup."

"I will leave," Bridget whispered. "Alone!"

"Don't be silly," her mother said.

"Yes, go away," Tom nodded.

"Nobody goes!" father shouted angrily. "We will go through this together. This was all a bad joke to frighten us—for whatever reason. As soon as we have the RV fixed, we will leave this place."

Suddenly a car stopped at the side of the road and a window opened. The driver looked like a farmer. He glanced at the huge palm tree and then at the overturned RV. "What happened here?" he asked, puzzled. "Can I help?"

"That is a long story," Mr. Knotterfield said. "My son got hurt. Could you take us to the next town?"

"Sure."

The farmer still looked confused. He squinted at the overturned RV. "All of you?" he asked skeptically. His car was too small for him, a family of four, and a dog.

"Only the two of you," Mrs. Knotterfield said, pointing to her husband and Tom. "I will wait here with Bridge."

"That's too dangerous."

"Towser will be with us."

Bridget slowly stood up and went towards the river. Suddenly it made no difference to her if there was a threatening tree man around. It did not matter if she got another hiccup or even if the monster wolf was nearby.

She just wanted to have peace.

"Where are you going?" her mother called.

But Bridget did not answer.

She ran towards the river, crying. *It is not your fault,* she told herself. *It isn't!* She stared at her reflection in the water.

She ran alongside the field and touched the stalks with her hand. She felt so alone, but still, she wanted to be alone now. She smelled the scent of barley and listened to the warm wind. Maybe she could just sit there and do nothing. Just wait and listen and smell the beauty of this terrible place.

She did not even bother to look for the tree man or expect to be hit by a stone. *This is going to end,* she decided. *The terrible hiccup will have to stop.* She heard the voices of her family shouting for her and Towser's barking. *They will take care of me. ha-ha,* she thought. *They promise that, but they can't do it.* She heard a door banging and a car leaving.

"Come back. That's dangerous!" she heard her mother's voice.

Was it really dangerous? Was the tree man still around? If only she was more powerful. She would grow a tree that chased the ugly tree man away.

She ran faster.

When she reached the palm trees, she gasped and sat down. The wind was playing with the huge leaves, and she realized that their colors were changing all the time. They turned red, purple, green, blue, and yellow and then red again.

Normally, she would have thought that this tree was

wonderful. But now she was responsible for the weird growth, she felt confused. She closed her eyes and remembered how she had built the tree man at home, together with Tom. They were friends back then, only a couple of weeks ago. The tree man had united them; now it was separating them.

What did all those doctors say? Hold your breath and think of something nice that you experienced the last days, or months, during the year. A nice party or a meal or something with friends or family. Just try to remember every detail.

She tried.

I will not breathe again until the danger of a hiccup is over, she decided. She became calmer.

She heard a noise behind her, but she did not care. She continued to hold her breath, eyes closed. She tried to remember a nice dessert she once ate on a birthday. *Whose birthday was it? Mandy's? Samantha's? Yes, it was a chocolate pudding with marzipan pastry. Hold on, there was something even more delicious than that, Walnut-vanilla tart. Yes, that was something her grandma used to bake when the kids came visiting.*

YUMMY!

"Bridge," she heard her mother's voice. Towser came near her and lowered his head, sniffing. She stroked his head and took a deep breath. *Is the hiccup gone now?* She could not say.

"Tom did not mean it," her mother tried. "He was scared and had a shock when the RV fell over."

"I know." Bridget closed her eyes again and tried to concentrate on hot wafers with cherries and cream.

And holding her breath.

Her mother sat next to her, and Towser strolled by the river. The dog was still excited after the strange events.

They sat without a word. *As soon as my hiccups are over we all might have a chance to lead a normal life again,* Bridget hoped. She thought about raspberry ice cream and the coconut cookies Mrs. Petersen brought as a reward when they all did well on the math test.

"Dad went to the next town with Tom." Her mother did not know what to say.

Bridget started breathing normally again. "I know." The hiccups were gone, for the time being, and the rushing water and rustling barley had a calming effect.

"You are a natural wonder, Bridget," her mother whispered after a while. "You give life to the trees."

"But I don't know if I still love trees. I do not want this power."

"I know, but look how colorful they are. These are fantasy trees. They are special!"

"Yes. But a lot of people hate me doing this. The neighbors, like Mr. Hillerman for example, and even some of my classmates. Now, even Tom! I am scaring people."

Her mother said, "You must admit that this whole

thing is extraordinary."

"But I do not want to be extraordinary," Bridget whined. "I just want to be a normal girl."

"You will be again shortly."

"I don't know." Bridget looked directly into her mother's eyes, searching for signs of disbelief. Adults sometimes say things to calm their kids.

But not her mother.

Bridget only saw confidence and belief in her mother's eyes. All will go away if we stick together as a family, her eyes seemed to say. Bridget laid her head on her mother's hip. She watched the big colorful leaves of the fantasy palm that seemed to shelter her. She even saw a coconut in the tree.

Finally, she closed her eyes again.

I am a natural wonder, she thought. *I am giving life to trees. What other eight-year-old could claim that? Yes, that is extraordinary.*

She must have fallen asleep.

When she woke up, her mother was daydreaming with Towser lying on her feet, snoring.

"Be careful!" Bridget suddenly cried. Her mother turned her head. A coconut fell from the palm tree and just missed her.

"Not hit by a stone but by a coconut," she breathed. They heard voices from the other side of the field and stood up slowly. Towser raised his head. "Dad is back," she said. "Let's go!"

"I'm staying here."

"No, you aren't." They heard a squeaking. Mrs. Knotterfield reached out her a hand and waited. Towser sniffed and vanished into the field.

Bridget looked around. *What if the tree men came back and find me here? Alone?* She would be scared even more. On the other hand, what if she caused even more harm to her family? An oak tree for their garden—okay. But what if an overturned RV and Tom's bruises were just the beginning?

Her mother smiled. "Don't worry, as soon as we are at Aunt Claire's you will find the rest and recovery you need."

Reluctantly, Bridget took her mother's hand and they went back to her father, Tom, and the damaged RV.

The Loggers Come Back

It was late afternoon.

Mr. Knotterfield was standing behind the overturned RV. Next to him stood a mechanic and a policeman. They all looked stressed and a bit clueless. The mechanic had brought a truck to tow the RV and bring it back onto its four wheels. In the truck was Tom, wearing a bandage around his head and looking annoyed. When he saw Bridget, he looked away.

"I have never seen something like this before," the mechanic said. He wore dungarees like the tree man's, only blue, a dirty shirt, and a cap with his company name on it. On his chest was a badge with a name: Don.

Bridget moved very carefully, trying not to be noticed. Her father looked at her for a moment too long.

"How did this happen?" the mechanic asked.

"I explained it already several times," her father answered, irritated. However, it was not easy to make such a scenario plausible. "I drove too fast into the parking spot, and . . . I simply underestimated the size of the bump with the tree growing on it."

"That was all caused by the tree man!" Tom shouted from the truck.

Don looked puzzled, but the policeman raised his hand. "Mr. Knotterfield, this is what you told us already," he said. "There were some kids in scarecrow costumes and—"

"It was a tree man," insisted Bridget. "They were throwing stones at us!"

"Yes! And they damaged my engine," added her father.

"But the engine could not be damaged because you 'underestimated' the hill?"

Mr. Knotterfield sighed. "Yes . . . I mean no, I guess."

"I need to write you a ticket first," the policeman said.

"*What*?"

"You drove too fast. That is what you said yourself. Otherwise you wouldn't have hit this palm tree."

"But it was by mistake!" Mr. Knotterfield tried to explain.

"I cannot remember that there were palm trees in this field." Don shook his head. "I know this field of barley very well. It belongs to my brother, Rick."

Bridget saw Tom rolling his eyes, and for the first

time in a long time, she smiled. She hoped that he didn't tell either the policeman or Don about her hiccup. That was a family secret.

"Can we start, please? We need to head off," she heard her father say.

"Sure. But we need some other hands to get this thing back on four wheels." Dan saw Mr. Knotterfield's reaction and added, "I will call the guys from the sawmill. They are working somewhere in this area. They might give us a hand."

Then he went back to his truck.

Ten minutes later a pickup arrived with several men in it. They were all loggers wearing jeans and T-shirts. One of them wore a long jacket and a wide-brimmed hat. He was the leader. Bridget recognized him at once. He was Ted Wood from Ted Wood's Wood Company. Oh no! That was the same company that cut the trees in the field at home. Ted and his bunch might remember about her secret powers, and the hiccups, and would surely tell the others.

Bridget did not like these people with their grinning smiles and dirty clothes. She assumed that it was their chainsaws she had heard before at the river. Before the stones hit her, her father, and Tom.

They came over to the RV, and Bridget realized Ted was watching her. "What do we have here?" he asked, looking at her. "Oh, what a wonderful palm tree! So strong and full of life! And there are two other ones. Incredible!"

"He underestimated the root of this tree and bounced against it," the policeman explained.

"Ah." Ted Wood laughed, not believing a single word. His men were smirking.

"That is all Bridge's fault," Tom said, approaching from Dan's truck.

"My son bumped his head," Mr. Knotterfield explained. "He is still in a shock, you know."

"What did you do with the stolen trees?" Bridget barged in.

Ted frowned. "We did not steal the trees! And we sold them to a furniture company."

Then somebody started a chain saw.

"No!" Ted said sharply. "We do not cut such a nice fantasy tree unless Dan's brother, Rick, gives permission." He eagerly looked at Dan who didn't reply. He simply turned away and began working to fix steel cables around the RV. The loggers helped him. Then Dan started up an engine on his truck, and the hydraulics strained. Soon the van was back on four wheels.

The family took a long look at the RV. It was scored with scratches and gouges and on one side there was a smashed panel. "The alternator cable was cut," Dan said. "But I can fix it."

"The tree men did that," Tom whispered.

"Maybe your son has seen some ghosts!" Ted laughed who heard it.

"*Ghosts*?" Tom and Bridget asked simultaneously.

"People are very superstitious up here," the policeman said. "Don't believe him."

Ted snorted scornfully.

"You mean the tree men were ghosts?" Bridget wondered.

"It's all superstition," the policeman said, and gave Mr. Knotterfield his speeding ticket. Bridget's father sighed and pushed it into his pocket.

Ted laughed again. *He knows the whole story,* Bridget thought, *so my powers are no secret anymore. Why didn't he or his men tell anyone? Maybe they thought no one would believe them.*

"What are you doing about the attacks from the tree men?" Tom asked. "Did you make a note on that? Will you chase them?"

"Sure," the policeman answered, smiling. "I got everything in my notebook here, little man. Drive carefully. And don't be superstitious!"

Then he left.

"Ghosts," Ted whispered mysteriously and looked at Bridget, who started to breathe quicker. Did he want to scare her?

"Let's go!" he shouted, and his men jumped into their truck. "We've got a lot of work to do!"

Bridget knew exactly what he was talking about: cutting trees. She hated this man. She watched them drive off, feeling a terrible uproar in her stomach again.

She hoped they would not owe Ted Wood a favor now.

Third Time is the Charm

"They will come back and cut these extraordinary palm trees," Bridget whispered when they all were gone. Only Dan was left, still working on the engine.

His lifted his head. "I will talk to my brother. These trees do not disturb anybody, so I guess he will leave them. Besides, they are wonderful. I am sure Rick will let them be."

"Would you ask him, sir, promise?"

He laughed. "Yes, I promise. I do not like these loggers. They are not from here but try to buy forests from the community to cut the trees. Not good."

Bridget was alarmed.

"Did you believe his story about the ghosts?" Tom asked, anxiously.

Dan did not reply at once. "No, but people are sometimes superstitious up here."

Ten minutes later he was ready with the engine and daubed with oil. "There we go. Works again!"

"Was it done on purpose?" Mrs. Knotterfield wanted to know.

"I don't know, but . . . well, to be honest, it was smoothly cut, so I guess it was not an animal. Whoever it was . . . " Dan shrugged, looking baffled.

Mr. Knotterfield paid the mechanic, who went back to his truck.

They all stood there, bewildered. They had been very lucky. Somebody wanted them to have a breakdown but why? Who would do something like that?

Bridget was frightened. *Somebody wants to kill us,* she thought. *A ghost? A tree man? The ghost of a tree man?* Whoever or whatever it was, the situation was dangerous. And the farther they drove, the greater the chance to see the monster wolf again.

Towser gave a deep bark. They did not have the time to think about kids and tricks and ghosts. Now they needed to hurry.

"Let's get out of here," Bridget's father said, and they all jumped into the RV. It started fine but rattled all the time and moved slowly.

"It won't take long now, kids. Maybe two hours," her father said and stepped on the gas. "I called Aunt Claire from the town and told her that we will be late."

"I am looking forward to a nice barbecue." Mrs. Knottefield smiled, trying to put everybody in a good mood again. "And a nice apple-vanilla ice cream."

That's what I was imagining when I held my breath, Bridget thought. *Apple-vanilla ice cream!* That is what she liked most. Aunt Claire had made it during her last visit to them a couple of months ago. "This is a family recipe," she had told them. "My great grandma tried it for the first time nearly a century ago."

The RV was rattling along as the highway passed through a spruce forest. Tom lay sleeping on his bed. He still wore the bandage around his forehead. Bridget wondered, *What will happen next?* She would have rather gone home, but was it safer there? People did not want her there either. Her hiccups caused too much trouble. She felt so lonely.

They finally passed a wooden sign with big letters that read "Welcome to Tretford's Apple Farm." Next to the letters was the picture of a juicy red apple. Tretford was Aunt Claire's last name.

They continued to drive through a forest, and Mr. Knotterfield said, "Only a few minutes left."

Aunt Claire

They saw the farmhouse from far off. Dusk was approaching and lights were switched on inside. It was a grey brick house with a tiled roof and green window shutters. The family drove under a strong wooden arch. Beyond it, a muddy path lined by apple trees led to the front door. Beside the house was a garage with a white pickup parked in front of it. Dozens of rows of apple trees grew in a large field behind the house and ended close to the forest bordering the property.

Aunt Claire sat outside on a wooden chair at a wooden table and peeled apples. Next to her on the muddy ground was a basket. She stood up when she saw the Knotterfield family arriving.

"Hello!" she shouted and waved. Bridget's father stopped the RV with a loud squeak.

"You are just in time for a great evening dinner!" she welcomed them. She wore an apron and a red dress with white dots on it. Her long black hair was pinned up, and she was smiling. Her nose and cheeks were red from the evening wind. She must have been sitting there for a while.

Bridget saw the wrinkles on her face. Something was bothering her. She was Bridget's mother's younger sister, but she looked older. Maybe it was after her husband's early death that she became more sorrowful.

Aunt Claire gave them all a hug. "Welcome to my farm!"

Bridget asked, "Did you prepare some apple-vanilla ice cream?"

Aunt Claire smiled cheerfully. "Wait and see. Look at your RV! What happened?"

"Well, we had a little accident," Mrs. Knotterfield said. "We'll explain over dinner."

Soon, they were in the middle of a great dinner in the dining room next to the kitchen. They sat around a wooden table and ate apple soup and red cabbage with apples and meat. A fire was spitting in the fireplace and on the walls hung historic photographs of the farm and some of Aunt Claire and her husband.

"Bridge makes fantasy trees grow," said Tom.

"It is not magic," Bridget explained. "I cannot perform miracles. Every time I get a hiccup, a wonderful tree grows."

They told her about the colorful trees in the field, the trees at school, and about the monster wolf, the tree men that were supposed to be ghosts or simply kids playing tricks, the broken tire and the toppled

RV, and, finally, about the colorful palm trees with the coconuts.

Aunt Claire frowned. "That sounds like an adventure."

"The doctors have recommended a recreation period for her," mother said. "A place she can rest and cure her hiccups."

"Well, this is the place to be then," Aunt Claire said. "Shall I show you around the house?" She'd already done this when they were here last time, three years ago. But she liked it, and a few things had changed since then.

Aunt Claire showed them her little kitchen with another fireplace, their tiny bedrooms on the first floor with double beds and huge cupboards, and a garden where she grew lettuce, carrots, cabbage, and several kinds of berries. Next to the garden was a field with little seedling trees. "This is where I grow a new field of apple trees," Aunt Claire said. "The apple picking season starts soon. In a couple of days, my workers come back from their break and help with the harvest. But we can start tomorrow if you like. What do you think?"

Tom muttered something, but Bridget agreed. That would be better than sitting around with her thoughts. Apple picking might keep her from thinking about her hiccups.

"I would rather go fishing," Tom said.

"Well, the little lake in the forest at the back of my farm is still there."

They went down a staircase into the cellar. "This is where the apples are pressed for my popular applesauce. The cider room." A lot of equipment for the apple harvest was there: some deseeding machinery, dozens of baskets, ladders, rakes, gloves, cord and wires, and some tall boots. It was dirty down there but interesting. Bridget did not remember the apple pressing machine from their last visit.

Aunt Claire went to a second room in the cellar. On the walls were many shelves with applesauce, apple wine, apple jam, apple tea, apple liqueur, and apple juice. The rest of the room was filled by a huge fridge. She opened it and took out a green box.

"Let's go and have some ice cream. I know, Tom, you don't like it. But I have apple pancakes with maple syrup and powdered sugar for you!"

"Great!"

"Is Henry still working for you?" Bridget's father asked.

"He is," Aunt Claire said, happily. "He is coming to see you tomorrow morning. Without him, I would not be able to manage all this." She sighed. "When Winston died, I was the one to take on the whole farm and the other land. There were many who wanted to buy it, but I refused. Look around! This is what we have done with the old farm. It's a flourishing business! Winston was always afraid of his lifework falling into the wrong hands."

They went upstairs to the dining room. Aunt Claire carried a tray from the kitchen, and on it were four bowls of apple-vanilla ice cream and one with an apple pancake for Tom.

Silently, they ate the delicious dessert.

"There is a lot going on in the woodlands farther north," Aunt Claire continued. "A timber company tries to buy forests from people here too."

"Ted Wood?" Mr. Knotterfield asked.

"Yes. Do you know him?"

"He helped us with the RV. And he was around our hometown after . . . well, to cut Bridge's fantasy trees!"

"That's far away from here," Aunt Claire said. "But he has a brother there working for the fire department."

"Did he want to buy this farm too?" Bridget's mother wanted to know.

"He tried."

Ghost Stories

After dessert they went upstairs to their rooms. They were very tired after the day of adventures. Tom and Bridget shared a room and so did their parents. "I want to sleep in my own room," Tom complained. "I do not want to wake up on top of a tree tomorrow morning!"

"Hey, I thought you like climbing trees," Bridget sneered.

"I need silence because of my head."

Luckily, Aunt Claire had another guest room free. It was smaller, but Tom was okay with it. Towser decided to stay in Bridget's room.

Bridget was tired. She fell asleep at once, and she did not dream of ghosts or tree men or monster wolfs but of a huge field of colored fantasy trees. All these trees were connected via tree houses and wooden suspension bridges. The kids from her school moved all over them, screaming, shouting, and climbing; they were having a lot of fun. She saw Samantha and Mandy in a hammock on a maple tree. Was that the one in their garden? Curt was climbing the highest tree to show off, as usual. And Lucas, Viv, and Patty stumbled over one of the bridges that connected two palm trees with coconuts. Everywhere were colors. The leaves and branches, the wooden bridges, and the trunks of the trees shone in red, purple, green, yellow, red, and even pink. It was wonderful.

Bridget climbed on one of the bridges and saw Mrs. Petersen sitting on a wooden platform in an old oak tree. She moved nearer, and her teacher turned her face towards her. "Don't scare her," she whispered.

What did that mean?

Bridget woke up and took a deep breath. It was just a dream, a bright, colorful dream. But then she heard the words again, "Don't scare her!"

The words came from downstairs, not from her dream.

Silently she jumped out of bed and gave Towser a sign to be quiet. Tiptoeing, she sneaked out of the door. It gave a squeaking noise, and she held her breath for a few seconds. She thought of the cracking noise of the stairs and lurked around a handrail upstairs. Her parents were talking low to Aunt Claire. They had not heard her bedroom door. She saw shadows moving in the dining room.

"—and I am just saying that some people still think that my husband Winston is walking around as a ghost to protect his property—and me," Aunt Claire just said.

Mrs. Knotterfield laughed. "That's ridiculous."

"I do not believe in ghost stories, as I said. That is all nonsense! It is just that people up here are superstitious. They do not come from a city like us!"

"You did not see what happened the last days when she had this terrible hiccup." That was the voice of her father. "So let's not scare the kids even more with ghost stories!"

"I cannot imagine her being supernatural," said Aunt Claire. "That all sounds pretty fantastic to me."

"I am just saying we have to be careful not to scare her."

"This is not a scary place."

"We all hope not . . ."

They moved to another room, and Bridget could not hear them. She stole back to her bed and tried to sleep, but she couldn't. What was this ghost story all about? Now she was afraid of being alone. She wished at least Tom was there. She was expecting a hiccup, but this time it did not come.

She remembered last night at the campsite when she sat on the steps of the RV and listened to the trees in the forest. Nearby Aunt Claire's farmhouse there was a nice lake. It was rather small, as she recalled from her last visit. Tom and her father would go fishing there tomorrow. It was a silent and cozy place. The Knotterfield family had a barbecue out there when she was four years old. She remembered enjoying it.

She imagined going there by night. She would be scared! She might glimpse a tree man or a ghost behind a bush or a trunk. Perhaps Uncle Winston? No way! That would make her hiccup—and then the woodland around the lake would be full of colored trees. By tomorrow, nobody would be able to find her and rescue her.

Truth was, she had to laugh thinking about that. Accept your power, something in her mind said. It will go away sooner or later anyway.

Towser snored. Bridget crawled out of her bed and went to a window with a view of the forest. The moonlight shone on the little field outside where Aunt Claire grew new apple tree seedlings.

Bridget stared at the rows of apple trees. She saw a shadow in one of the rows. What was that, a *ghost*? The shadow moved slowly and clumsily. It had long thin arms sticking straight out from the body, nearly right-angled. Bridget held her breath. Was it a scarecrow blowing left and right in the wind? Or maybe it was—no! She saw the shadow moving towards the light and—there it was! Quickly she moved away from the window.

She suppressed a cry.

Towser was awake immediately and looked suspicious. Bridget ran directly downstairs, ignoring the cracking of the stairs. Her parents and Aunt Claire were sitting in front of the house chatting. When they saw her appear in the doorway, they were alarmed.

"A tree man!" she cried. "It's the one that attacked us in the field of barley!"

"Bridge that was a dream," her father said, standing

up and hugging her.

"It was real," Bridget said. "Somebody is following us!"

Her father said, "Don't worry. I will have a look, promise. No need to be anxious." But Bridget could hear her father's heart thumping hard and fast.

"Where was it?" her mother asked, grabbing her hand.

"Between the apple trees!"

Her parents looked puzzled, not believing it. Nevertheless, her father went to the RV and came back with a flashlight "Stay inside," he told them. Then he ran into the field with Aunt Claire and Towser following.

Soon Bridget and her mother saw the pale circles of the flashlights between the trees.

It was silent then—*hic, hic!*

Bridget thought she heard the rumble that announced the growing of a new fantasy tree. Or was it just her gut feeling? Her stomach roaring?

She went back to her bedroom, and her mother quickly closed the window and the shutters. "Don't be afraid," she said, hugging Bridget. It was completely dark in the room now. Her mother quickly switched on a little light on the nightstand and sat down by her side. Then they waited, with her mother gently stroking her hair.

After an endless time, they heard father and Aunt Claire return. They came straight up to Bridget's room.

"We saw nothing," he said, puzzled.

"If there was a tree man, it's gone now," Aunt Claire added.

Her father gave her a kiss on the cheek and went out of the room with Aunt Claire.

"I will stay here until you sleep," her mother said. Bridget nodded and closed her eyes. Everything was quiet again. She was quiet again. Finally, she fell asleep with her mother still stroking her hair.

Thuja Plicata

The next morning, it seemed obvious that nothing had happened.

Bridget stared out the window but could not see any new colored fantasy tree that had grown overnight. However, she wondered about that because she knew she had hiccupped after the strange glimpse of the tree man. Where was the tree?

For a few minutes, she was happy. She thought her supernatural capabilities were gone and the hiccup last night was only super-normal.

At breakfast Aunt Claire asked, "So who will join me picking apples?"

Bridget was happy to join her and enjoy the fresh air. Her mother wanted to go for a walk and join later, and Tom wanted to go fishing with their father. Nobody spoke a word about last night.

Bridget put on boots and old clothes she got from Aunt Claire and took a ladder out to the field. Her aunt helped her carry it. They passed the little field with the new stalks of apple trees. Suddenly they heard a roaring from far off. A small car was trying to drive to the entrance arch. And then they saw it.

The arch was broken, and the reason was— "A tree, look!" Aunt Claire said, dumbfounded and confused.

Bridget saw a big oak tree standing right next to the arch. The car was struggling around it to get back on the driveway again. The oak had a red trunk and purple and yellow leaves. It looked out of place beside all the apple trees. Immediately, Bridget was sad again. So there it was—the tree that was born last night after her hiccup.

"I am so sorry," she said.

"That's unbelievable!" said Aunt Claire. "How could such a thing happen?"

The car approached. It was at least a hundred years old and rattled. Bridget recognized Henry behind the wheel. Bridget hugged herself. *What will Henry think of the tree? Of me? Of my powers? Will he still like me?* She hoped so.

Henry parked the car and climbed out. He looked just like Bridget remembered. Henry had always been old. His hair was grey, and his skin was weather beaten because he worked on farms all his life. He wore an old straw hat, ripped jeans, and a shirt that once was white. He smiled all the time and had a happy face that usually turned even happier when he saw Bridget.

However, today he only looked startled.

"Good morning," he greeted and raised his straw hat. "I don't remember such a nice tree standing at the arch when I left yesterday."

Aunt Claire shook her head. "No, it wasn't. Long story! You are early today, Henry."

"That is because the kids were coming!"

Now he finally smiled, and Bridget let her breath out. Henry opened his long arms and gave Bridget a big hug. Then Tom came out of the door with their parents and also got his hug. He was still wearing his bandage. It looked cooler, he thought.

"Can anybody tell me what's going on here?" Henry wanted to know.

They all sat down at the wooden table and explained everything that had happened. Aunt Claire went into the kitchen and came back with mugs of chocolate.

Henry was puzzled. "You are supernatural, Bridge," he said. "Wow, I know a supernatural little girl. That's wonderful!"

Bridget shrugged. "I do not really like it so much."

"At least she likes the trees she creates," her mother added, smiling.

"Well, time for work now. Bridge and I will go to the field," Aunt Claire said. "You want to join, Henry?"

"Sure." Henry nodded, still puzzled.

Shortly afterwards, Mr. Knotterfield and Tom drove off in Aunt Claire's pickup, curving carefully around the colorful fantasy oak tree at the entrance. Mrs. Knotterfield went for a walk, and Henry and Bridget climbed up the ladder to pick apples. Below them, under the tree, they had put a couple of baskets. Aunt Claire stood by another tree in another row. The sun was shining, and the day was warm. Only a very light wind was blowing. *It will be a wonderful and relaxing day,* Bridget thought.

No hiccups, please!

"Have you really seen this monster wolf?" Henry asked softly. He was careful not to make her scared again just thinking about it.

"Yes. And I do not want to see him again!"

"Clear. But how come a wolf is somewhere around your area? They are not often here."

"So no wolf is around here, you think?" asked Bridget.

"None. Never seen one at this time of the year, and I have lived here since my birth."

Later they played a game she'd learned from Henry when she was here the first time. It was about aiming for the basket with an apple. As soon as an apple was picked it had to be thrown into the basket. If it hit the basket, it was one point for Henry (as he was more trained) and three points for Bridget. The one who first had a basket filled won.

"The apples will be bumped if I throw them into the basket," Bridget had said at first.

"It doesn't matter. With these apples, Aunt Claire is making her famous applesauce," Henry had explained.

So they started. They nearly had a second basket filled when father and Tom returned from Fincher's farm. They were both carrying their fishing rods and bait and heading towards the forest.

"We will let you know when we have enough fish to make everybody happy," Tom said, smiling. Mrs. Knotterfield came back from her short walk and helped Aunt Claire at the other tree.

Bridget threw an apple into the basket. The score was 29 to 21.

"I think it was a ghost that I saw last night," Bridget told Henry. She needed to hurry to catch up with him. He nearly had his basket filled with apples.

Henry was amused. "A *ghost*? Well, there are no ghosts!"

"But I have seen it. It was a tree man. But suddenly he was gone. It must have been a ghost."

Henry laughed and threw an apple at the basket but missed. "Look around, and tell me what you see."

"What do you mean?" An apple was flying into the basket. It was now 30 to 27.

"There are a lot of hiding places here, a lot of trees that throw their shadows. It might look like a ghost moving in the darkness when the trees move their branches back and forth. I personally do not believe in ghosts."

"You don't?"

"No. However, people up here are sometimes superstitious. But honestly, I already caught some kids playing scarecrow one day."

"That is scary." She picked an apple and threw it. 30 to 30.

"It is funny! Kids like dressing up sometimes. You know that. Wearing these costumes of, let's say, a scarecrow or, well, a tree man! Look, Bridge, if everything I've heard is true, you have a very extraordinary capability. You can grow the most colorful fantasy trees. That is magic. I am nearly seventy years old, and I have never seen that in my life."

"But I do not feel comfortable with it. I do not really like it."

"Maybe you would if the growing of those trees were not caused by a hiccup."

"It happens only when I am scared," she whispered. "And I do not want to be scared!"

Henry nodded. "I know. Nobody wants to be scared."

"Aunt Claire talked about a ghost last night. She said Uncle Winston is going around here in the fields."

Henry looked up and threw an apple. 31 to 30. "Your uncle is *dead*. He cannot walk around. Please, Bridget, promise me not to be scared by these ugly stories."

Bridget thought Henry must know what he was talking about. He'd lived here for a long, long time. She believed he didn't say that only to calm her down. If she were able to grow whatever tree she wanted to grow just by moving her hand, or thinking about it, it would be a special present. *That* would be magic, as Henry called it, even more because she loved trees so much. The weird thing was that the fantasy trees only grow when she was scared. She picked an apple and tossed it into the basket. 31 to 33. Yeah!

Suddenly she heard Tom's voice from the forest. "Come to the lake!" he shouted. "You must see this!"

They walked down the trail that led to the small lake. Around it were bushes and trees. The shoreline was usually sandy and muddy in some places, but now it seemed to be underwater.

Was the lake flooding its banks?

Father was sitting on a rock, staring at a huge tree standing in the middle of the lake. It had beautiful leaves in different shades of red and green and a golden trunk with red lines in the bark. It looked as if it was standing on an island. The tree was very tall and had a huge trunk. "A giant cedar," Tom said, admiringly. He was still carrying his fishhook. "That one is great, the nicest and strongest I have ever seen. Thanks, Bridge!"

The hiccup last night, Bridget thought, *it not only grew the oak tree at the entrance arch but also this gigantic cedar.*

"Where did that come from?" Aunt Claire asked, coming along the trail. She looked stunned. *"Thuja plicata!"*

"What?"

"That is the name of this tree. You only find them in a few spots here in Canada—or even worldwide! They are the biggest on earth. People call them the *tree of life.*"

She paused. Everybody was silent now, looking at the giant in front of them.

"It's wonderful!" Bridget's mother said.

"Perfect!" her father added.

"That is magic power." Tom sighed. "I want to climb on it. We could build a bridge to it."

Then they all looked at Bridget at the same time. Bridget did not want to meet their eyes.

Instead, she turned and ran back to the house. She was sitting beside the fireplace in the dining room when Henry and her mother found her. "Leave me alone!" she cried.

Aunt Claire appeared at the door and said, "That is the most wonderful tree on the whole property. It takes ages—or should I say hundreds of years—to grow and you made it in only one night."

Now she seemed to believe the miracle of Bridget. The girl was *special*.

"Claire," Henry said, "that lake is not your property. It belongs to the Thomson's."

"Maybe I'll buy it from them."

Mr. Knotterfield and Tom put their fishing tackle in a

corner. They had not even started fishing. Poor Tom!

"The tree is not so far away from the shore. We can build a bridge and have a picnic underneath it," Tom suggested. He did not seem to be bored anymore. This could be an adventure.

"You okay with that, Bridge?" her father asked, carefully.

She raised her head and looked at her father and then at her brother. They all really liked the gigantic life tree on the lake's "island." Nevertheless, Bridget wanted to get away from here. She needed time to think about all this.

"Sure," she said. "But, Mom and I will go to town and buy the things for the picnic. I need to go . . . somewhere."

"Agreed." Her mother smiled.

"So then we all know what to do," Henry summarized and clapped his huge hands. "Mrs. Knotterfield and Bridge will go to town, Mr. Knotterfield and I will build the bridge to the island, and Tom will go fishing for the barbecue."

"Take my car," Aunt Claire offered.

"Bring some chocolate donuts," Tom begged.

"And eggs for a pancake," Henry added.

"Then also bring maple syrup and cream," father said.

"And sausages." That came from Aunt Claire and Tom simultaneously.

Bridget took some notes and started off with her mother in Aunt Claire's car. They stopped by the new oak at the entrance arch. It was like the one in their garden at home. The leaves shone in the sun, and Bridget marveled at how beautiful it was. The arch was broken at one side but would be easy to repair. *A wooden arch can be fixed,* Bridget thought, *but a tree that is cut cannot be put back together.*

Mother asked, "You okay?"

"Yes," Bridget said, but she wasn't entirely sure.

She liked all these wonderful trees she was creating, but somehow, it was all so frightening. If she was scared, the trees would grow. If she was not, she was scared about her hiccups coming back. It was a vicious cycle.

They drove on through a forest to a supermarket. It had big windows, and they could see inside. It was filled with people. *They must come from all over the area,* Bridget thought. They grabbed a shopping cart and went inside.

They bought all the things for a nice barbecue by the lake—and even more. They bought eggs for Henry, maple syrup and cream for Bridget's father, chocolate donuts and sausages for Tom, biscuits, cheese, potatoes, meat, tomatoes, and lemon juice. It seemed that the only thing they did not buy were apples. And fish.

While they stood in a long line for the cashier, Bridget noticed a car parking on the other side of the road. It was a van with golden letters on the side: Ted Wood's Wood Company. It was standing directly in front of the police station. She saw Ted coming out of the station. He was joined by a policeman. It was not the one they met yesterday after their breakdown, the one who gave her father a ticket for driving too fast. Ted shook hands with the policeman before driving away.

As Bridget and her mother drove back, Bridget opened the window for fresh air. After a while she heard the familiar noise of a chainsaw somewhere deep in the woods. Ted Wood's van was standing on the road shoulder, and nearby, a logging truck was parked with a load of logs.

They carried on silently.

"Do you think that Aunt Claire has money enough to buy the forest behind her property?" Bridget asked after a while.

"I don't know," her mother said. "Let's ask her."

"We should persuade her to buy it. If she doesn't, eventually the men will cut my beautiful tree."

"I am sure they won't. It is a life tree!"

Bridget did not answer. Soon they saw the sign of Tretford's farm with the apple on it. Later, they passed the broken arch and the oak tree. Bridget's mother curved around it and got on the driveway to the house.

Mrs. Knotterfield parked, and they unloaded their groceries and then found Aunt Claire sitting under an apple tree eating—an apple! She was groaning. "I will be glad when my workers come back next week. My back hurts."

"Is Dad still at the lake?" Bridget wanted to know.

"He is building the bridge with Henry."

"I will help them," Bridget said.

"There is an apple cake in the kitchen. Take it with you for the picnic. I will take your bag."

Bridget went to the kitchen. She'd just grabbed the cake when she heard the noise of a car.

Aunt Claire's Farm is Not for Sale

Ted Wood's van was curving around the arch. Aunt Claire stood up, looking troubled. Ted parked behind Henry's old car, and he and Gary climbed out.

"A wonderful good morning, Miss Tretford, Mrs. Knotterfield," Ted greeted. "Nice tree you got out there, must have cost you a fortune!" He pointed back to the arch and the colorful oak tree.

"Fast growing trees are quite common around here recently, I heard," Gary snickered.

Bridget watched them through the kitchen window, which she'd opened to hear the conversation.

"What do you want?" Aunt Claire asked brusquely.

"Did you think about my offer?"

"Ted, I told you I won't sell."

"Well, I have made an offer to buy the bush behind your farm and I thought—"

"You will not get my farm," Aunt Claire insisted. "Even if you buy everything around it."

"Why so stubborn? I think the price is good."

"The price is bad, you know! You only want to cut those lovely trees."

"But that is my job, I am afraid. We can make an arrangement that if I have cut everything, I will sell it back to you again, and you can plant some nice apple trees. What do you think? *Deal*?"

Bridget had enough. She was closing the kitchen window again when it squeaked.

"Ah, did I see the tree witch girl?" said Ted. "I am sure the oak tree at the entrance is her work."

"We do not know what you are talking about," Mrs. Knotterfield intervened angrily. "Please leave at once!"

Before Ted could answer, Bridget appeared at the door and stood there for a moment.

Ted's eyes gleamed. "I could use an employee like you, little girl," he said. "Tell me your price!"

"Have a nice day, Ted," Aunt Claire said coldly.

He nodded, gave a friendly wave, and returned to his car with Gary strolling behind him. A minute later they were on their way.

Bridget's mother was angry. She looked at her sister who was just standing there, watching Ted's van disappear. "So you have *already* got an offer to sell the farm?" The sisters glared at each other.

Meanwhile, down at the lake, Mr. Knotterfield and Henry were building the bridge to the island with the giant cedar tree. They were wearing rubber boots and carrying big heavy stones to put into the water.

Henry was groaning. "That is not good for my back." But he was smiling.

Mr. Knotterfield was sweating. Towser barked happily. They'd already created a path of single stones that led to the island. It was nothing more than a small hill on which the cedar tree was standing. However, they would have room for the barbecue.

Tom sat on the island, fishing. He had taken away his bandage. At the edge of his forehead was a red bruise but nothing serious. He'd exaggerated his severe injury. As always. In the basket next to him were some fish he'd caught.

Bridget came and swiftly jumped over the stones to the island, carrying the apple cake. Towser sniffed but quickly lost interest. He did not like sweet things. Mother and Aunt Claire were following with the grocery bags, but then Mrs. Knotterfield turned and vanished again on the path.

Bridget sat down next to Tom. "Hush," he said, "the fish will hear you."

Bridget stared up. Above her head, the cedar's

strong branches, with reddish shaggy bark, waved. Wind sang through their colorful fronds. "This tree is really beautiful."

"And large. Father said the oldest one is more than fourteen hundred years old."

"Help your aunt over the bridge," Henry instructed the kids. Aunt Claire was already balancing over the stones. Quickly, Tom and Bridget went to carry grocery bags for her.

Henry heaved the last stone into place. He called it the shore stone. It was the first one that a person had to step on to reach the island from the lakeshore.

Mrs. Knotterfield arrived with blankets and a jug of tea. She spread the blanket with Tom's help, and then Aunt Claire and Bridget spread the picnic food on it.

"What shall we call the bridge?" Mother asked.

"What about *Hiccup Bridge*?" Tom suggested. They laughed.

"You are mean," Bridget answered, but smiled. Somehow, she liked the name.

Bridget realized that her mother avoided looking at Aunt Claire. She was angry, and Bridget knew why. Bridget asked, "Will you sell the farm?"

Aunt Claire sighed. "That was never my plan."

"But what happens if Ted Wood buys this bush with the lake in it?" she insisted.

"Nothing will happen. I will stay on my property."

"But this giant life tree will be removed!" Bridget said.

Aunt Claire sighed again. "Ted is trying to buy a lot of property up here. But most people declined his offers. This area belongs to the Thomson family. They have a farm on the other side of the forest. Mick Thomson, their oldest son, is our local police deputy."

Bridget remembered the policeman in front of the office this morning who was shaking hands with Ted

Wood. But she did not say anything.

"We need to buy and keep the giant tree," Tom said.

"I do not have so much money," Aunt Claire said.

Bridget stood up and went back over the bridge.

"Where are you going?" her mother asked.

"We forgot the dessert, apple-vanilla ice cream!"

"I will join you," her mother called. "I need to make the omelets."

Henry was happy. "I love omelets! Thank you so much, Mrs. Knotterfield." A few seconds later, Bridget and her mother hurried along the trail.

Ghost Attack

They went back to the kitchen in the farmhouse and—on their way—grabbed an apple from one of the trees.

"I will make the omelets," Bridget's mother said. "You take the ice cream back to the others. Don't wait for me."

Bridget went into the cellar and to the room with the huge fridge. It was cold and dark, so she switched on the light, found the ice cream and an apple pancake for Tom, and made her way back upstairs towards the picnic.

As she headed back through the rows of apple trees, she saw a movement.

What was that? Something was flashing across the row of apple trees she was walking through. She stopped and listened, but she could not hear anything. The sun shone warmly on her face, and a light wind blew. Maybe it was the branch of a tree swaying. She slowly moved on.

Suddenly, between other apple trees, she saw movement again. It was not a branch of a tree blowing in the wind; it was a tree man! And it was standing right in front of her.

The tree man was wearing red dungarees, the yellow shirt, and the straw hat. A broad grin was painted on the wooden face. The head wiggled. The tree man stood with its arms widely stretched open, like a cross. It looked weird, especially when it was moving. But now it was *not* moving. It was just staring at her.

Bridget was terrified. She stopped dead in her tracks and stared back at the strange stature. The tree man started walking towards her.

"What do you want from me?" Bridget shouted, gasping. The tree man wiggled its head and giggled. Her stomach clenched in terror.

She ran.

She heard a whisper. "Bridget!" For a moment, she thought it was coming from the apple trees around her. She entered another row. Was that a ghost? Uncle Winston in the shape of a tree man? Again, she heard her name being whispered.

"Mom!" she cried, running.

Suddenly, a second tree man appeared behind another apple tree. It was wearing green pants and a red shirt. Hold on—a second tree man? So there really was more than one? Bridget sprinted in a zigzag course through several rows of apple trees. Only the wind was blowing.

A third tree man appeared, wearing purple dungarees and a white shirt. The heads of all three wiggled at the same time.

Bridget ran to the right. Where was she? She ran to the left, still gripping the ice cream and the pancake. "Bridget!" She'd heard the whisper now three times from three different tree men.

"Wait for us!"

She did not wait but ran. How many were there? And who was hiding behind those terrible masks? If they were ghosts, why are they chasing her?

"Mom, Dad!"

Fear grew bigger and bigger inside Bridget until, finally, the hiccup burst from her. *HIC hic hiccup hic!* It did not stop, and she did not stop running. *Don't look back,* she thought.

Hic!

She ran and ran, and her eyes sight was blurring. Then she bent over behind an apple tree to catch her breath. She dared to cast a quick glance into the field but could not see the tree men, so she continued onwards. A roaring was blustering behind her. Somewhere a new tree was growing, but hopefully not at the farmhouse, endangering her mother.

Hic!

It was getting worse. She heard a gunshot and stopped abruptly. The shot did not come from the lake where her family was having the picnic. It came from the farmhouse. Then another shot. For a moment, Bridget thought of climbing up one of the apple trees to hide, but she was too frightened to do so. She continued running.

And running.

She ran until she finally bumped into someone behind another tree. It was her father.

Towser came barking into the field of apple trees. He was trying to follow the tree men who had vanished.

"You okay, Bridge?" her father asked.

She gasped. "The tree men! Three of them were following me!"

Everyone else arrived in a rush.

Henry hugged Bridget. "All will be good," he whispered. Meanwhile, her mother ran into the field again with her father and Aunt Claire following, all very angry.

Hic!

In the distance, there was still the roaring noise. Henry sat down with Bridget on the muddy path.

"Come out, you cowards!" her mother yelled.

"You terrible tree men, show yourselves!" Aunt Claire hollered.

"We will soon have a whole new forest here," Tom complained. He looked anxious. "I don't want your mighty power any more. It attracts too many strange creatures!"

He was right.

The roaring was overwhelming now. Then Aunt Claire screamed, "Look! My new field of apple trees!"

"Where are you, you crook?" Mrs. Knotterfield shouted again, but she did not get a reply. Only Towser's barking was heard. Then Bridget heard a voice she had never heard before. Somebody said, "Is everything all right?"

Then, suddenly, there was silence.

Henry, Tom, and Bridget all stared at the apple trees. No one was to be seen. Suddenly, Mr. Knotterfield appeared and waved. "All is good now." He disappeared again and—seconds later—rushed in their direction. "Constable Dinkins is there," he said.

"Are the tree men gone?" Bridget asked.

"I don't know. Towser is still chasing them."

They all stood in front of Aunt Claire's new apple trees. The little seedlings were gone. Instead, there were five new apple trees, with yellow, red, and purple leaves, full of green apples.

"This is a dream, right?" Aunt Claire could not believe what she saw. "I thought I had to wait a couple of years until I got my first apples from these trees." She shook her head and then turned to meet Constable Dinkins' eyes. "This is a good friend of mine," she said. "Once in a while, he visits me to see if everything is okay."

Dinkins was a tall man with a clean blue uniform, a mustache, and brown, dense hair. He did not understand anything that was going on. His mouth was wide open. Henry picked an apple and gave it to him. "Try it."

Dinkins took it and looked at the apple suspiciously. "So it is true," he said.

"Where did the gunshot come from?" Tom asked, still looking frightened.

"From my gun," replied the constable. "I heard a cry for help and fired some shots into the air. What happened?"

Mr. Knotterfield told Sheriff Dinkins the whole story. Dinkins did not give a sign whether he believed it or not. He just listened. Finally, he said, "Honestly, it is a strange story and hard to believe." What father did not tell Dinkins was how it all began with the monster wolf in the field behind their house. "Tree men," Dinkins resumed. "Hmm, maybe it was just somebody dressed up like a scarecrow?"

"NO, THEY WERE TREE MEN!" Bridget shouted so loud that even the trees shook.

Immediately, there was silence.

Even the constable did not say another word. After a while, he said: "Well, the gun shots must have dispersed the . . . whoever they were!"

But where did they escape to? wondered Bridget.

"People are talking," Dinkins continued. "I heard they talking about a little girl who is able to grow trees in record time. I did not believe it I must say."

Well, it was hard to believe, wasn`t it?

"How do people already know about Bridget?" Henry asked.

Bridget was suspicious. "Was it Ted Wood?" she asked.

The constable nodded. "I guess he was one of the first ones I heard it from, yes."

Suddenly they heard Towser growling. He trotted back from the field carrying a big piece of cloth in his mouth.

It was green with some red dots on it. "Blood!" Mr. Knotterfield said. "This is proof that these terrible tree men are human."

Aunt Claire said, "Constable Dinkins, thank you so much for coming. You really need to do something about these attacks. My family is scared. They all think there are ghosts out there attacking them. We do not even know the reason why."

Then they smelled it, something burning. "The omelets!" Mother cried and rushed into the kitchen.

"Let's go back to the lake," Henry suggested.

"I will do some new omelets," mother promised.

At least their picnic site was still untouched. When they arrived at the giant cedar tree, Constable Dinkins, who'd joined them for a cup of coffee, was again amazed. "Wow, is that a *Thuja plicata*?"

"It is," Aunt Claire said proudly.

Dinkins looked at the colorful leaves and the strong branches. He noticed that two of them were parallel. "You can build a tree house on there, kids," he said, smiling.

Bridget and Tom did not answer. Bridget was eating ice cream, and Tom was munching pancake. "Ted wants to buy my farm," Aunt Claire explained.

"He wants to buy a lot of farms out here," Dinkins said. "Truth is, he is about to buy the forest behind your farm too. The contract is ready to be signed soon, I heard. They gave him permission to check out the trees in this forest already. Ted wants to mark some areas of trees to be cut soon."

"*When?*"

"He wants to start tomorrow."

"*What?*" Bridget couldn't believe her ears. *No!* They'd start tomorrow? She heard the terrible noise of the chainsaw roaring and gasped. *Calm down*, she told herself. "But this giant life tree must stay," she whispered.

Constable Dinkins looked puzzled. "He wants to open a big timber yard up here to transport all his wood to other places. That is what my deputy, Thomson, told me."

"But that would kill my farm. The noise, the dirt and oil smell and all . . ." Aunt Claire shouted.

"That is the reason why he made you an offer." Mr. Knotterfield understood now. "The offer will definitely be lower after he has bought this forest."

They were silent until mother brought the omelets. But nobody was hungry anymore.

Mr. Knotterfield gave the piece of cloth to Dinkins. "This is the proof that somebody wants to frighten us," he said. "Not tree men, not ghosts, but humans. Find out who that is, constable!"

"Ted Wood," Bridget muttered.

Her father was exasperated. "They use the superstition of the people up here to scare them. Do you know if other farmers around have had similar encounters with, well, tree men? Or other '*ghosts*'?"

Sheriff Dinkins shook his head. "No, not as far as I know, but I will ask around."

"Do that! If they have scared the farmers with

their ghost stories, nobody will want to work here anymore. Then they can easily buy the farms. Maybe this is what happened with the Thomson's."

"I will investigate it," Dinkins said and stood up. Then he returned to his patrol car.

He had not even touched his cup of coffee.

Making Plans

"Ted Wood comes from the south," Henry said. "His family is still living down there. Ted has bought large forests farther north and down here and continues doing that. We do not know where his money is coming from, but obviously, he has enough."

Aunt Claire sighed. "The community also sold land to him that they shouldn't have."

"Then we need to stop him," Mr. Knotterfield said.

"How?" Aunt Claire sighed yet again. "Honestly, I

would do that, but it does not give me anything back. What would I do with a forest full of other trees? Only my apple trees give me income."

"But the forest is home to animals and protects your farm from the wind and snow and is a nesting place for birds," Bridget said. "It smells nice, and it makes oxygen for us to breathe."

Aunt Claire nodded. "You're right. I am curious why the Thomson's sold it to Ted Wood."

"Why didn't they ask *you* to buy it first?"

"They did, but I said no."

"So, it is not so easy," Mrs. Knotterfield said. "Do we know how much the Thomson's want for the forest?"

"I did not ask them."

"Please do," Bridget begged.

"Maybe . . ."

I have an idea, Bridget suddenly thought but did not

say anything. She knew she must do something even if it was risky—and *scary*! She sat next to Tom and grabbed a chocolate donut from the picnic basket. Then she whispered in his ear.

Her brother shrugged. "I am not sure."

"Think about it," she said.

Later that evening, after Bridget had gone to bed, she sneaked out of her room and over to Tom's. She tapped at his door. "It's me, Bridge," she breathed. A couple of seconds later the door opened and Tom's face appeared.

"Let me in. I need to talk to you."

Reluctantly, he opened the door, and she stepped in. "Did you think about my idea? We need to do something, Tom," she urged. "We need to prevent the giant tree from being cut. And, I mean, the whole forest."

"How do you want to do that?" her brother asked. "Collect signatures again?"

"I told you this afternoon! Forgot?"

"Building a tree house?" he asked doubtfully. "A few kids won't stop loggers from cutting trees!"

Bridget shrugged. "We did it once at school, remember? Let's try again. We build the tree house in the giant life tree at the lake! It has two parallel branches that are strong enough."

"But that is not your tree," Tom insisted.

"But I created it," she said proudly. "What do you think?"

"That will never work." Tom sighed.

"It will," she said. "I am sure."

But was she? It's a way to fight my fears and the hiccups, she thought. *Or to make it all worse!*

Early in the morning, even before breakfast, she started off. Tom was still in bed. If he did not want to help her—fine! She would manage alone. She took Towser to protect her.

According to Henry and Aunt Claire, there are no monster wolves around. No ghosts either—the tree men seemed to be human as they had found out, thanks to Towser. *What else?* she wondered. *Wild animals? Hmmm, they do not come out during daytime, do they? And Towser will hear and smell them.* In the cellar, Bridget looked for things she needed to build the tree house. Then she quickly made her way out to the field and passed the new line of young apple trees that she grew yesterday.

Soon, she reached the path to the lake. Stopping, she stared into the forest. If there were tree men lurking around, Towser would have snarled. She went on to the lake and jumped over the heavy stones of the Hiccup Bridge and finally stood under the giant cedar tree.

She could only hear the noise of the trees blowing in the wind. Her heart pattered. *I am still a little scared,* she admitted to herself. *But I must do this!* For a long time, she stood watching the shadow of the giant cedar tree with its colorful fronds that shone in the sunlight. She discovered the two parallel branches, which were not very high. She could easily get there.

A perfect place to build a tree house.

She jumped back over the Hiccup Bridge and started to collect sticks and branches. She brought them to the giant tree and fixed them together with a piece of rope. Then she climbed up the tree, holding the end of the rope in her hand. As soon as she reached the two branches, she sat down and pulled the bundle up.

Suddenly, Towser made a noise. Wood cracked and somebody came through the undergrowth. The dog barked, but it was a happy bark. Tom arrived carrying a few more sticks and a basket.

"Thought I would bring some breakfast." He grinned.

He came over the Hiccup Bridge and gave her his bundle of sticks and after that the basket. Then he took a deep breath and climbed up to sit down by her side, gasping.

She lined the sticks next to each other on the two strong branches of the tree and fixed them with the rope. Tom helped her. At the end, the tree house looked like a little platform that was strong enough to sit on and wait for Ted Wood and his bunch.

"Do Mom and Dad know we are here?"

"Yes. I told them we are going to have breakfast at the giant cedar tree."

"They didn't mind?"

"No. I told them you were here already. I thought they would say no. They are so worried about you."

Does Tom sound envious? wondered Bridget.

She opened the basket and found eggs, toast, jam, cheese, and donuts. In a thermos, she found hot chocolate. She took two cups out of the basket and filled them with hot chocolate and threw a piece of ham to Towser, who was resting at the tree's base. *This is a wonderful beginning to the day,* she thought. *No hiccups and a nice breakfast in a tree house with my brother. No arguments. No tree men. No monster wolf, and no ghosts. Hopefully, the day's end will be as good.*

Then they waited—but no one arrived except their father.

"Will you come and help us with the apple picking?" he asked.

"But the loggers will kill the tree."

"If the Thomson's sold this forest to Ted Wood, he can do what he likes with it." Then Mr. Knotterfield took a closer look. "This tree house looks like a watching platform."

"We watch the forest for intruders," Tom agreed, and Towser yelped.

Their father sighed. "Perhaps we can ask Mr. Wood to let this beautiful tree stay where it is. Now please come with me." Not a convincing argument, but Bridget and Tom had to obey. Grumpily, they climbed down the tree.

"Look at you! So dirty!" their father said, throwing his hands up in horror. Indeed, they were completely messy. Their clothes were covered in green smudges and brown stains. Bits of cedar frond stuck to them.

Even a small twig was tangled in Bridget's hair. The kids giggled, and Bridget saw Tom wink at her when they crossed the Hiccup Bridge. Their father carried the breakfast basket, not saying a word. *Tom and I now have a mission,* Bridget thought. *A mission that makes us close again.*

They worked the whole day picking apples, always listening for the noise of a chainsaw that did not come. In their breaks, they ran to the giant cedar just to be around it or to have lunch. Henry came later that day, and they played the apple target game again with Tom joining in. By midday it was 547 points for Henry, 483 for Tom, and 528 for Bridget.

So many apples.

During the afternoon, they caught themselves glancing towards the forest every couple of seconds. They could not help it. They were nervous. Where were those loggers? Nobody arrived, and no chainsaws ran. Had Constable Dinkins managed to keep Ted and his bunch from clearing the forest?

In the middle of the afternoon, Tom climbed down

his ladder and went to his father who was picking apples with Aunt Claire and his mother in a parallel row.

"I don't want to pick anymore," he said. To be honest he was fed up with picking apples. He showed his full basket and smiled. "Can we go back to the tree house?"

Mr. Knotterfield smiled back and looked at his wife. She nodded. "All right, you did a lot of work today, my son. Go, but take Towser with you."

They took their baskets into the cider room and went back to the tree house. The giant cedar stood in the glade like a lighthouse. The sun shone on its colorful fronds. The tree house platform was the same as when they had left it that morning. Nobody had been there. That was strange. Didn't the loggers want to begin marking the trees to be cut today?

"I have another idea for how we can chase them away," Tom suddenly said. "At least from this forest."

His sister was hooked. "How?"

He told her.

A bit later, they stood back in the cider room and looked at all the tools that were used during harvest and after to prepare Aunt Claire's famous applesauce, apple wine, apple jam, apple juice, and so on.

It smelled like cider and rotten apples. They saw buckets, rakes, shovels, ladders, and dozens of baskets. In the old cupboard standing against one wall they found wires, cord, glue, screws, hammers, and even an old bear trap.

There was a thick layer of dust on some of the tools, which had not been used for a long time. Towser sneezed, and soon after, they left carrying a lot of stuff. They would need to make two trips to the cedar tree.

Bridget heard their parents talking in one of the rows. They were taking a break and drinking tea or a glass of Aunt Claire's nice apple liqueur. They must think the kids were on their tree house platform and Towser was with them.

Bridget and Tom sneaked towards the path. When they were finally there, they giggled conspiratorially.

This was all so exciting.

"Don't get too excited," Tom warned. "Otherwise the hiccups will come back."

"I have no fear," Bridget said proudly. And that was the plain truth. Yes, she would be excited if all they were planning worked out.

Nobody disturbed them for the next two hours. They had everything prepared when it was time for dinner. The sun was still shining but soon dusk would fall. Their father was calling them, so they left their new favorite place at the lakeside and went back to the farmhouse. A light shone in the dining room.

"Get changed and ready for dinner," their father shouted when he heard them coming. He could not see them, which was good because they were even dirtier than that morning. They also heard Henry's voice; he was joining them for dinner. "Let's eat outside. It is still very warm."

Quickly, Tom and Bridget vanished upstairs and changed.

"Don't tell them anything," Bridget warned her brother before dinner. She knew he was very quick to blurt out secrets.

"Did you have a rest on the giant cedar tree?" Henry wondered as they ate turkey.

The kids nodded. Yes! Bridget was not tired; she felt wide awake. And excited.

"Something must have held Ted Wood back today," said Aunt Claire. "I am sure he will come tomorrow, and we will wake up to the noise of a chainsaw."

"Did you find out about the price for the forest?" Bridget asked her aunt.

"Yes. I can't afford it."

Not good at all.

Soon after dessert, Bridget stood up and rubbed her eyes. She pretended to be tired, and to be honest, she was indeed tired.

"I am going to bed," she announced and gave Tom a kick under the table.

"Me too," her brother quickly said.

Mother said, "You do not have to help us tomorrow morning. I know how much you like the giant cedar tree. Go there as long as this logger is coming." She did not even mention Ted's name any more.

"Let's make him an offer to save this one tree," their father suggested. "What do you think?"

"You would do that?" Bridget was happy to hear this news.

"We might buy it if needed."

Bridget looked around at her family and Henry. Everybody was nodding. If the giant cedar tree on the little island was saved, it was better than not saving any trees at all. It was a very special one. A life tree. *Eventually that will stop them from their plans,* Bridget thought. *Only if—*

"You can ask Ted directly if you like," Henry threw in. "Look! Here he comes."

The van with the big golden letters curved around

the arch and the tree and approached the house.

A light wind was blowing. The loggers got out the car and came to the wooden table where the family sat.

"Good evening, all," Ted opened, sounding friendly. Obviously, he was in a hurry. "This is the last time I am going to ask you. I wanted to inform you that this morning I signed the contract to buy the forest behind your property. The contract has only to be countersigned by Michael Thomson."

"The policeman?" Henry asked.

"Correct."

"Congratulations," Mr. Knotterfield sneered.

Ted grinned proudly. "So, did you think about my offer?"

"I am *not* going to sell my farm," Aunt Claire said clearly. Her eyes left no doubt about it.

Ted looked disappointed. Gary looked scornful. "Well, is that your final word?"

"Yes, it is. But I would like to ask you to sell the giant cedar tree to me."

Ted was amused. "You mean the new tree on the new island?"

"Correct!"

"I cannot sell it to you."

Bridget felt a sudden kick in her stomach. But this was not because another hiccup was coming.

"Why *not*? What do you want to do with that one tree?" her father wanted to know.

"Well, it is a very beautiful fantasy tree, I agree, but still, it is a tree that brings more money than all the others. So it will be cut!"

"*No!*" Bridget's cry simply burst out. Tears welled in her eyes. "You cannot do that, Mr. Wood! Please!"

"Well, young lady, who will stop me, eh? At least you can grow new trees at home, can't you? With your extraordinary capabilities! Only a little fear and a new tree is here, right?" He laughed out loud.

Bridget looked at her parents for help.

"We will pay you the price you might get for the wood of the tree," her father offered, "plus ten percent more!"

Ted grinned smugly. "Honestly, I do not even know how much I would get for the wood of such a tree," he said. "So what is the offer?"

"Tell me a price!"

Ted thought for a moment. Then he sighed inconsolably. "The answer is no. I will cut all the trees, understand?"

"We could make an arrangement to—" Mrs. Knotterfield started to say, but Ted put his finger on his mouth and shook his head.

"Hush! You hear me? We will start cutting the trees. My contract with the Thomson's is almost complete. When it is signed tomorrow, nobody can stop me cutting the giant cedar tree."

Bridget glared at Ted's back as he turned to leave.

"We will see about that," she muttered.

Trapped

Mr. Knotterfield saw his daughter's bewilderment. "Don't worry," he said. "Don't get agitated."

"I won't," she promised.

"This man is a nightmare," Aunt Claire said.

Then there was silence; they were unable to put their failure in words. They had just lost the giant cedar tree.

"Maybe he is bluffing," Aunt Claire finally said. "We all know his methods—or at least have a suspicion. Perhaps Constable Dinkins will find proof that Ted and his bunch put people under pressure to sell their properties by making them scared! If that is the case, the whole contract will be obsolete."

"But still, there is no proof yet."

"I do not want Ted Wood as our neighbor," Henry groaned.

"It is too late," Tom muttered. He started cleaning the table.

Bridget frowned with concentration. *I know what I must do now,* she thought. *I need to set a trap for the tree men. I need to entice them out. Come out of your hiding place to scare me! This is the only way I can save the cedar tree. How can I do that? By getting scared and having a hiccup.*

Yes, you have read correctly. She needed to be *scared*! It was risky but as simple as that! She wanted to prove her suspicion was right. If so, the true people behind the masks of the tree men would be exposed.

And she was pretty sure she knew who it was.

The next morning, she woke up when it was still dark outside. She went to the window and opened the shutters. The forest was silent. In the other room, her father was snoring. She sneaked out of the room, taking Towser with her. She gave him a sign to be quiet.

She knocked at Tom's door, and he opened it. "Let's get ready," she murmured. "Either you come with me now or don't come." She turned, not willing to wait another minute.

"Wait. I will come!"

He got dressed slowly, but finally, they tiptoed downstairs with Towser following. They opened the door and sneaked outside. A fresh wind blew. First morning light would show the way to the lake. They listened.

"Are wolves out there?" Tom asked.

"No." Bridget was sure.

"Bears?"

"Maybe."

"*Ghosts?*"

No answer.

The ripe apples smelled sweet and mixed with the scent of the forest. *Today, I will manage to save the forest,* Bridget thought. *And my extraordinary hiccups will help me. I am good. Nothing will happen to me. Only fear!*

How weird that was. As soon as they reached the tree house, which looked like a watching platform, they climbed up and made themselves comfortable. Towser lay down at the base of the trunk and stayed there.

Bridget had brought a blanket they spread over the platform. Next to them there was a basket they had filled with old rotten apples from the ground. They sat still, waiting.

"They will come, I am sure," Bridget said to her brother. "I will go and check everything again. Will you stay here?"

"Sure. Or maybe I join you?"

Bridget rolled her eyes. "No. Stay here and secure the tree house."

"Aye, aye, madam." Tom saluted. "Be careful!"

She laughed and took Towser with her. They went down to the lakeshore, and Bridget checked the little hole in the ground. It was a trap.

Bridget felt a little grunt in her stomach.

She was nervous. But she had to be strong now. She went down the main path and turned right onto the smaller path leading into the dark forest. She walked for a couple of minutes and listened, but there was only the noise of the trees.

Moving farther away from the giant cedar tree, she checked a few other traps in the woods. Then she climbed into some low hanging branches in a tree and checked a rope that was connected to a bucket.

All was ready.

She climbed down again and checked another rope that was hidden under a bunch of leaves. She nodded, satisfied. Turning, she jumped and then froze in fear.

Right in front of her, not even ten meters away, a shadow appeared. A *tree man*! The creature was standing behind a bush. It wore green pants and an ugly purple shirt. The head was a terrible wooden mask with a grinning grimace. On top was the well-known old straw hat.

"Hello, Bridget." She heard a whisper, but the creature did not move. Not even the head was wiggling. Its arms were spread wide from its body. "Are you *scared*?"

"What do you want?" Bridget cried.

She was far away from the giant cedar and Aunt Claire's field of apple trees. Nobody would hear her shouting. Towser was barking, but Bridget held his collar tight. She felt the grunt in her stomach growing stronger. The tree man just stood there, not moving. Like a ghost.

"I am . . . not scared," she tried, but her voice was not really convincing. *Scare me,* she thought. *I am mighty, and I have magic capabilities. I can create fantasy trees that smash you out of my way.* Yes! All of a sudden, she felt strong but not completely secure. She was still frightened of these creatures. She heard laughter from where the tree man stood, but it still did not move. She took a stone from the ground and threw it at the creature. No movement, only a dull bump when the stone hit it.

"You. Do. Not. Scare. Me," she repeated slowly and firmly and threw a second stone.

Towser was leaping, and she let him go. Suddenly, the tree man fell over. Towser was barking angrily. The whole thing was not real; it was only a wooden figure. But who had spoken to her before?

She wanted to head back to the tree house, but she realized another shadow was behind her. And that one was certainly moving!

"Hi, Bridget, let's create some new fantasy trees," she heard a voice say. "We need some more!"

Then she saw the other creature. It looked completely the same as the wooden one that just fell down. But this one was moving slowly towards her. Its arms were stiff, made of thin branches that looked like a cross. She stepped backwards.

"Leave me alone!" she gasped.

"You have such an extraordinary talent, little girl," the tree man said. Its branch arms were still not moving, but its head was wiggling. Man, how she hated the wiggling of that wooden head!

"Let's make some more trees in this fancy forest," the tree man whispered.

"Go away!"

Towser was still barking, but she stepped back and grabbed his collar, holding him tight and keeping him from jumping towards the creature. She did not want him to get hurt.

As the tree man moved in her direction, it crossed an invisible rope fixed underneath the leaves on the ground. The rope was connected to the bucket in the tree above. The bucket was filled with cold water from the lake, and as soon as the tree man crossed the rope, the water was tipped over it.

"Aaaarrrgh!" the creature shrieked. "That is soooooooo cold!"

The bucket fell right over the creature's head, covering its ugly mask, and it could not see anything. It staggered from side to side and finally barged into a tree.

Bridget used the moment to escape. She heard a metallic clang from the bucket when the creature bumped against another tree.

"*Hmmmmmpf,*" it grunted.

Quickly, she pulled Towser out of the danger zone and deeper into the forest.

Am I going the right way? she wondered as she rushed along, jumping over roots, dodging low branches, and slipping on ferns. Her heart hammered. Everything in the forest looked the same.

Suddenly, hair rose on her neck as something howled. The sound echoed amongst the dark masses of trees. Bridget did not have time to figure out where it came from. Another tree man—the one from farmer Rick`s field of barley in red dungarees, yellow shirt, muddy jacket and straw hat— appeared at exactly the point where—hold on! That was the next trap! Bridget stopped abruptly and moved towards the tree man.

"I will get you," she heard a whisper. "Oops!"

The creature was tumbling in. *The trap worked,* Bridget thought in relief. She and Tom had placed a ladder under scrub, leaves, and mud. Between the rungs of the ladder they had dug shallow holes. The tree man had now stepped in one of those holes, his tree arms stretched out.

"What is *that?*" It toddled a few clumsy steps forward—and tumbled. A pair of truly human hands appeared from under the shirt, bracing the figure against its fall. "*Ouch!*"

Bridget heard a voice very far away and thought it was Tom's, shouting for her. She moved forward, trying to pull Towser away from the tree man. "I will come get you, little tree witch!" the tree man yelled, still trapped in the ladder. But the creature was strong, and soon it got free again and chased her.

Bridget ran away, jumping over rocks. Within a few seconds, the tree man was back on her track. She ran between two bushes, but the tree man quickly caught up. *Thud, thud, thud* went his boots and *thud, thud, thud* went Bridget's heart.

BANGGGG!

The creature stepped onto a shovel that was lying on the path between the bushes. Its handle smacked into his grimacing face, and he tumbled again. "*Yeeeouch!*" he hollered. He did not stand up again.

"Bridget, wow, well done," came a murmur. A third tree man appeared from the underbrush. "*Uuuuuaaaa!*" He moaned like a ghost.

Man, how many were they? Bridget's pulse raced,

and her hands sweated. Fear was growing inside her, clutching her chest, her stomach. Here it came, rising up her throat!

Hic!

She heard a rumble right next to her and bolted away as Towser barked even louder. The tree man chasing her wore blue pants and a dirty yellow shirt. His face was rigid with fear. She felt the grumble inside her stomach again and gasped.

Then she let Towser go. "*Attack!*"

The dog lunged towards the tree man, and she ran in the other direction. When he saw the dog coming, the tree man began to scramble away. "Help! A monster is chasing me!" the man yelled. Hiding behind a tree, Bridget heard another thud and Towser's barking, mixed with the noise of ripping cloth.

"Bridge, where are you?" shrieked Tom, sounding scared.

She sprinted towards his voice. "I am on—*hic!*— my way!" she cried. "The tree men—*hic!*—are following me."

"Yes, and soon we will get you!" snarled a voice behind her. She saw the yellow-pants tree man catching up quickly.

The rumble became louder.

"The trees are coming," she heard Tom's voice say. Then a loud roaring came from where her brother was. What was happening? Did they start to cut the giant cedar tree already? But, it was not the noise of a chainsaw.

She could see the giant tree in the distance. Then she heard a howling again. Was it a wolf? Oh no! But listen—it sounded weird, like—

"*Uuuuuuaaaahhooooooooo!*"

A second later, she reached the lakeshore. Tom waved from in the tree. He was still sitting on the platform, crying. Although the tree men had not bothered him, he was too frightened to call for their parents.

She gave him a sign. "Be quiet!"

Then she saw it. Beside the giant cedar tree was a second smaller one. It also had strong, dark-red branches and yellow leaves.

Thuja plicata.

"Quick!" Tom said. "Let's get out of here." Then his gaze fastened on something behind Bridget. She looked back. Behind her stood the wet tree man in green pants and the ugly purple shirt. He was carrying a chainsaw in two human hands that appeared under his outfit.

"Now I got you!" the tree man shouted, crazy with anger. Where did he suddenly get this chainsaw from? The creature must have struggled free from the bucket of water. It was ready to attack again.

Bridget quickly jumped over the stones of the Hiccup Bridge with the tree man pounding after her. But on the second big stone, he slipped. The chainsaw fell to one side, and the tree man plunged to the other. *RRRRATATATATATUUUUUUUUU!*

Some of the stones of the Hiccup Bridge were spread with soap. They were very slippery.

Splash!

The tree man was wet again! The creature fought to get out of the water. The terrible mask floated on the lake, and a human face was revealed.

It was Gary's.

The Dark Corridor

Bridget climbed up the tree and saw her brother's scared face. "These are not ghosts. They are humans!" she said reassuringly.

They wanted to frighten me to get more of the fantasy trees to cut down, Bridget thought. Ted Wood had given away his secret by bragging about how much money he got from fantasy trees. Gary hauled his terrible chainsaw out of the water and waded alongside the slippery Hiccup Bridge. He was wet anyway, so he did not care. He struggled to start the wet saw, which choked and spluttered, belching out blue smoke.

"Now you are trapped," he yelled, moving towards the bottom of the trunk. Did he really want to cut the tree while Bridget and Tom were sitting in it?

His face contorted with fury as he yanked on the saw's starter cord again. Bridget and Tom pelted Gary with rotten apples. *Patsch!* They rained onto his shoulders.

Patsch!

The logger dumped his chainsaw and tried to climb the tree. His wet boots slipped. More and more rotten apples hailed down on him. But he did not stop.

"*Ugh!*" he cried, climbing farther. His face and body were smeared with apple sauce. It looked weird as he was still wearing his tree man outfit, arms straight.

"We need to get out of here," Tom repeated. "*Quick!*"

Bridget nodded. "Let's go climb down the other tree." She pointed to the cedar tree next to their giant one. It was standing in the water, but its strong branches would be able to hold the two of them.

"Kids, are you okay?" their father's voice called from very far away. "I heard a noise!"

"No!" they yelled simultaneously.

Bridget heard the howling from the deep woods again, and then felt another grumble in her stomach. *Oh no, not now,* she thought. *The other tree man will be here soon. Our mission has failed.*

She and Tom crawled to the end of the platform just as Gary's hands grasped the other end. Tom climbed across two limbs from two different trees.

"I am scared!" he cried.

Hic! Yes, me too, she thought. "Let's hurry!"

Below them was the silent water of the lake. She heard Towser somewhere in the forest.

Gary shimmied out along a limb. His weight made

it bounce up and down. Suddenly, with a load crack, the limb broke beneath Gary and fell into the lake.

"*Help*!" he cried.

The kids quickly climbed down the other tree and jumped to the shore. The tree man in blue pants ran away from Towser at the other side of the lake. There was a big hole in his pants.

"Get this monster away from me!" he shouted. He ran towards the Hiccup Bridge. Before reaching it, he stumbled, and his feet slipped into a little hole. "*Ugh*! What the—"

The hole that Tom and Bridget had dug was not deep. They'd filled it with rotten apple sauce and rotten apples. It smelled disgusting. The tree man tried to get out of the apple slobber. Then Towser was at his side, growling and keeping him trapped there. This gave Tom and Bridget time to run back to the apple field.

"*Uuuuaaaah*!" Two other creatures jumped onto the trail in front of them, one with the red dungarees, the yellow shirt, the muddy jacket and the straw hat.

That is definitely the one we'd encountered during our breakdown, Bridget thought. The other wore yellow dungarees and a blue shirt.

"You can run, you can hide, I will take you for a ride!" the yellow tree man sang.

The red creature beamed with joy. "So many trees! We want a whole new fantasy tree forest from you, little Bridget!"

"You will—*hic!*—not frighten me!" Bridget shouted.

"We did already, ha-ha!"

"Scary little lady, scary little Bridget," the yellow one sang.

Bridget turned. Where was Towser? He was still with the other tree man at the lakeside. She grabbed her brother's hand and escaped down the path back into the dark forest. How could they get back to the field? They raced along.

"I am coming!" Their father and Henry shouted from far off.

With a rumble, another tree began to grow, flinging mud aside. Within seconds, a wonderful apple tree with a yellow trunk and light green leaves rose from the ground. The yellow-shirted tree man bumped against it. *BANG!*

"*Owww-oooo!*"

He howled like a wolf, which scared Bridget even more. The creature tried to stand up again, staggering around, disoriented.

"Let's go," she whispered and dragged her brother deeper into the forest.

"Where are you?" their mother shouted. They heard Towser barking. The red creature in the muddy jacket was right behind them now, its skinny tree arms reaching for Bridget's flying hair. But, suddenly, a red trunk came from the ground and took the shape of another apple tree with green fruit on it. The tree man was trapped in its branches and lifted skywards.

"Help!" the muddy man shouted, throwing up some human arms. "Get me down from here!" He struggled in the tree.

The yellow tree man was watching with his mouth open. He was still in a daze and could not make any move.

Bridget grabbed an apple. It looked juicy and fresh, but that did not interest her at the moment. She needed it as a missile.

"Get this cheeky girl and the boy," the muddy man commanded, spluttering.

The yellow one woke from his daze and caught up quickly. In the meantime, Bridget and Tom had moved to the most dangerous place in the whole wood. The tree men, however, could not know that.

Bridget looked around carefully. *There's the cedar tree,* she thought. *And there's the baby spruce. So our dangerous trap is right over there.* "Stand very still," she told Tom. Suddenly, she could not help laughing. The hiccups were gone for the moment.

"You are cheaters!" Tom cried back.

"No, we are not," the yellow tree man argued. "But it is good that everyone thinks we are *ghosts*, right?"

"Was it Ted Wood who wanted you to dress up like that?" Bridget shouted.

"Watch your mouth!"

She took a bite into the apple and then threw it at the creature.

"Hey, that *hurts*! Just you wait, little girl!" The creature stepped forward. That was the moment she was waiting for.

Crack.

The snare trap tightened around the man's leg. "*Owwww-OOOOO!*" His howling was deafening. He pulled out a knife to cut the snare wire.

Hic!

She grabbed Tom and ran again while another apple tree grew from the ground.

But the apple tree had made a slippery hole as it thrust from the ground. Bridget's sneakers slipped, and her body pitched off balance. As if on a slide, she and Tom slid into the hole. They ended up in what seemed to be an old cellar or corridor, with a muddy concrete floor. The rumbling noise of the apple tree stopped. Soon, they saw the ugly wooden mask of red muddy man at the top of the hole.

Where did he come from so quickly?

Slowly, the creature slithered down to them with a big grin. Suddenly, the three others appeared behind him. There was the one with the red dungarees and the one with the white shirt and the purple one that ran from Towser. Finally, there was Gary, carrying his chainsaw. The sun was shining onto their backs as they entered the hole. They became silhouettes, and their stiff wooden arms and wiggling heads were more frightening.

"Now tell me, Bridget, what scares you most?" muddy man's voice asked.

"Go away," Tom mumbled, terrified and gripping his sister's hand.

"Noth—*hic!*—ing!"

The tree men laughed, and Gary quickly put on

another mask. It was an ugly wolf's head. "Does that scare you, Bridget?" he asked gleefully.

Hic! It did.

The creatures laughed. "What an awesome noise," muddy man shouted. "Well, people were talking in your home town. I heard you are afraid of wolves!"

"Yes, that's what he heard!" the yellow tree man said.

They laughed even louder now. They were howling. "*Uuuuhuuuuuuuuuuuh!* Your parents will not find you. *Uuuuuuhuuuuuuuuuuh!*"

Tom said, "I will call my dog!"

"Shut up!" spat the one that had been trapped in the snare. "I am not finished with you yet. *Ouch!*"

A roaring noise came from inside the corridor where it was dark. Soon a root cut its way through the concrete and suddenly a little light shone into the cellar.

The tree men howled.

The root scratched its way around all sides of the concrete wall of the cellar. Another root appeared at the other side, farther away.

How could they get out of here?

There were only two ways. The first was blocked by the tree men at the entrance of the hole. The second was more uncertain. It led into the darkness. But hold on—the light shone through little holes the roots created. Bridget stood up and dragged her brother with her. "Come on!"

"I do not want to go in that dark corridor," Tom murmured. "Where are Mom and Dad?"

"*Uuuuuuhuuuuuh!*"

"My fantasy trees are giving us light!" Bridget was convinced. "We cannot go back, so there is no other way!" Then she ran, holding her brother's hand tightly.

Tom cried, "No! We will be buried under the mud!"

CRRRRCK. New roots came from everywhere along

the cellar walls. The little lights shone in various spots and showed them the way forward.

Bridget stopped for a moment and looked at the roots on both sides. She remembered the oak tree root at the school entrance back home. "Wow, look how big these roots are!"

For a moment, she was amazed.

"Follow them!" she heard muddy man's voice behind them.

Bridget and Tom ran on through the corridor. Left and right, the roaring noise of the roots drove them towards the unknown. More and more light burst into the corridor, and it seemed the roots were following them. But muddy man's bunch was also after them.

"Scary little lady, scary little Bridget!" they yelled, their words echoing from the dark walls.

Suddenly they heard Towser barking somewhere behind them, and one of the tree men crying, "Not this monster dog again!"

"We are coming!" That was their mother's voice. She and father must have found the cellar entrance and were running through the corridor.

Then something mysterious happened. The kids seemed to be grabbed by one of the roots that were crawling along the wall.

"Hold on tight!" Bridget screamed as they were lifted up, sitting on the root. Again, they cried for help, but the roaring of the growing roots was too loud. Nobody answered.

The hard cement ceiling was cracking apart, revealing dirt above. *We will be squashed by mud,* Bridget thought in panic. They could not move, and they were still being lifted up.

The mud opened, and a golden light warmed their faces. Like in an elevator, they were lifted higher and higher, directly out of the dark cellar. They burst into open air, sitting on the branches of a big apple tree!

Hic!

The tree had a golden trunk, similar to the giant cedar tree at the lake and leaves in all colors. It shimmered in the sun. Bridget and Tom immediately stopped screaming, amazed by all the colors. "Help!" the tree men yelled somewhere behind them—no, not behind them! They were *below* them. From belt buckles and shirt sleeves, they dangled, caught in the branches with eyes wide. They kicked and swung, struggling to release themselves.

Lifted higher in no time, soon they hung like Christmas tree decorations, just a couple of branches lower than Bridget and Tom. Their stiff wooden arms were wiggling straight from their shoulders, making them teeter up and down with no chance to grab the branches and free themselves. They tried to free themselves with their human hands under their costumes and then tried to get to the tree trunk but without success. They were still wearing their wooden masks, with the exception of Gary, who had put on the wolf's mask. They all looked weird and freaky, but their heads were not wiggling anymore and were instead looking up the tree.

"Let me down!" one of them yelled

"I suffer from vertigo!" another tree man cried.

"I swear, you'll be sorry for this!" Gary grunted.

"*Ouch*! My whole body hurts," the one that stepped into the trap whined. "Get me a doctor!"

At the same time, Bridget heard Towser barking.

"Get this monster away," the tree man in the blue pants shouted. "Otherwise I am not coming dooooooooooooooown!"

He was actually the one hanging on the lowest branch. When it cracked he fell directly in front of the dog who was scrabbling out of the hole in the ground.

Next to the big apple tree was the hole in the ground that they'd come from. It revealed another entrance to the underground corridor. Bridget tried to look around. Several big apple trees had been growing since her last hiccup in the corridor. They were standing in a line from the forest to a little field and ended with the big apple tree they were all hanging on. On the other side of the field was a red farmhouse.

Nearby she spotted two people. Their mouths were wide open with amazement, but their eyes looked scared. One of them was a young man wearing a policeman's uniform; the other was an old lady in a flowery dress and with a walking cane. Bridget recognized the policeman again. It was Deputy Thomson.

Her parents appeared out of the hole in the ground, their faces agitated. Mrs. Knotterfield was frantic. "God, what happened?"

"Kids, what are you doing in that tree?" their father asked.

Constable Dinkins came too, with Aunt Claire and Henry following. They all stood staring at the tree in complete bewilderment.

"This is freaky!" Constable Dinkins said.

His deputy woke up from his amazement, and glanced at his boss. "What . . . uh . . . are you doing here?"

It sounded like a silly question considering the whole scenario. "I tried to catch some ghosts," the constable said, "and I think I have found them."

"Let me down at once!" muddy man shouted angrily. He was not on a higher branch of the apple tree and was fidgeting the most. The result was a loud *CRRRRRCK* followed by a swish and another crack. Then the branch broke and muddy man fell to the ground with a loud cry.

"*Heeeeeeeeeeeeelp!*"

With a big bump, he landed on the field and his wooden arms snapped. His mask fell off and revealed a human face.

The face of Ted Wood, boss of the logging crew.

Who's Fooling Whom?

"What is this all about?" the old lady asked croakily. "Mr. Wood, what are you doing in that silly outfit?"

She was following Deputy Thomson to the big apple tree. "Was that an earthquake?" he asked.

"No," Mrs. Knotterfield said, "definitely not."

"Let's get a ladder and bring my kids down," Mr.

Knotterfield urged. Constable Dinkins sent his deputy off for a ladder.

"Hey, what about us?" Gary shouted.

"We will not help you unless we all know what is going on," Constable Dinkins explained. "You have heard Mrs. Thomson's question!"

"I just came to get your signed contract," Ted Wood said.

"It does not look like it," Mrs. Thomson said.

Bridget could not help laughing. First, it was just a giggle, but then she burst out loudly. The hiccups were over, the situation was cleared, and she was crawling carefully along the branch of the tree. She could maybe get down without a ladder. Tom was still in shock and not able to move. He held tight to the branch he was sitting on, whining anxiously. This was definitely too much for him.

"Stay where you are, Tom," mother shouted. "Bridge, what are you doing? Wait for the ladder!"

As she crawled along the branch, it dipped down, and she jumped lightly to the ground. Her father and Deputy Thomson came with a ladder, which Mr. Knotterfield climbed to fetch Tom. Mrs. Knotterfield hugged her children tight.

Ten minutes later they all stood under the giant maple tree. "Take off your masks," Aunt Claire commanded.

Ted Wood and his bunch were revealed. Their faces were upset, and most of their wooden arms were broken. They smelled terribly of cider or stagnant water. They were wet and sweaty. One of them was still whining, the one that had stepped into the snare trap.

Tom was pale and did not say a word. *At least no one seems mad at us,* thought Bridget. *Our plan to show the "ghosts" were loggers worked in the end.*

"So," Constable Dinkins started. "What did you think you were doing?"

"We are innocent," Ted protested. "We can do what we want in *our* forest!"

"That is not your forest," Dinkins grumbled.

"It is still ours," Mrs. Thomson croaked. "My son and I wanted to sell it to Ted Wood, but now we need to think it over again."

"*What?*" Ted could not believe his ears. "These kids thought we were ghosts and set us up. Look at us! They hazed us! You should arrest *them*!"

"Yes, these kids are dangerous," Gary moaned, his clothes still dripping.

"Liar!" Tom cried.

"So why did you dress up like a tree man?" Mr. Knotterfield asked. He was beside himself with rage. This was all too much. His kids had revealed the whole plot, and obviously they'd been in danger. "Why did you pretend to be ghosts?"

Dinkins said, "Many other people in the area were fooled too, I found out. You wanted to frighten these people to make them sell their land, right?"

Ted Woods did not answer. Finally, the man that had

stepped into the snare trap had enough. He wanted to get out of that weird situation and see a doctor as soon as possible. "We wanted to frighten these kids before we started cutting the trees," he confessed.

"Shut up!" Ted Wood shouted.

"So our suspicion was right," Henry claimed. "You wanted to get more of those fantasy trees growing in that forest?"

There was silence until old Mrs. Thomson declared, "I will not sell my forest to you anymore."

Ted Wood looked up. "But, you signed it!"

"No, not yet," Deputy Thomson said. "And we won't."

Aunt Claire suddenly stepped in. "You can sell it to me then."

"*You*?" Mrs. Thomson asked.

"Why not? I mean, there are a lot of new apple trees in that forest now, so eventually they will belong to my farm."

Mrs. Knotterfield added, "Yes. We will put our money together and buy the apple tree forest."

"We will continue this discussion in my office," Constable Dinkins said. "Deputy Thomson, please help me bring this bunch back to town."

The Monster Wolf

"It will be great if we can afford to buy this forest!" Bridget said. She hugged herself happily. *I was scared, but I was brave too,* she thought. *And so was Tom! Together, we foiled Ted's evil plot.*

Mrs. Thomson smiled at Bridget. She agreed to a lower price that even Aunt Claire and her parents could afford to pay. Their families had been good neighbors for years so why not offer them a deal?

"That's great! We will come more often now to visit our giant cedar tree," Bridget promised.

"Only the tree?" Aunt Claire asked, pretending to be offended.

The next days went by without any hectic events or hiccups. Indeed, Bridget was not frightened anymore and had a lot of time to rest and relax. *My hiccups vanished in that last big hic when the apple tree appeared from nowhere and lifted us up from the dark corridor,* she thought.

"That was an old buried culvert that took water to fields around here," her father found out. "Nobody knew it was still there."

Bridget decided to give the big apple tree to the Thomson family as a present. She did not really express that it was a present because the tree was already standing on their property, so it belonged to them anyway. But it was a good thank you, so she asked old Mrs. Thomson to keep an eye on the tree.

"That is the most colorful apple tree I have seen in my life," Mrs. Thomson said. "I am very old already, but this one surprised me so much. Well, I will watch it with eagle eyes, I promise!"

They went to the tree in the lake nearly every day, and if they were hungry, they picked apples in the forest. Tom was happy again. He recovered from what happened, and even better, he respected Bridget's powers. They had a lot of fun between the apple trees and the forest that was now owned by their aunt.

The only thing they did not do again was build another tree man.

One night soon after the capture of Ted and his men, Bridget again heard howling outside. For a second she felt a clutch of fear. Would her hiccups return?

But it sounds like a wolf for real, she thought. *Henry says he hasn't seen wolves in this area lately . . . She did not want to find out and stayed inside the house.*

A week passed, and the hiccups did not return. It was almost the end of the summer, and her parents decided it was time to go home. Bridget thought of their promise to Mayor Richardson. No other fantasy trees would grow on the field.

Well, let's see, she thought. She suddenly had a good feeling that the hiccups were over, once and for all. It did not mean that she would never get a hiccup again in her life, but they would only be normal ones. Why did she have that feeling? *My extraordinary capabilities are over,* she thought. *Now that I've finally got used to them.*

Everyone hugged goodbye, and the family set out on the long drive home. When they passed Rick's field of barley, they saw the palm trees still standing there. Dan had kept his promise to ask his brother Rick to keep the trees. Even more, he had made a business out of the fantasy palms.

Dan parked in the space at the little bridge. Next to it was a booth selling coconut drinks. The mechanic was sitting behind it and serving drinks to another family that had stopped.

Mrs. Knotterfield shook her head and laughed. "Let's

take a break and get some fresh palm tree drinks!"

"Not here again," Tom murmured, carefully watching the field of barley. But no tree man appeared.

They all got their drinks. Bridget was curious about how coconut milk directly from a fantasy palm would taste.

It was smooth, sweet, and cool!

They journeyed on and stopped for the night at a RV park. Early the next morning, when Mr. Knotterfield started the RV again, the engine rattled and quickly died. "Not again," mother sighed.

Bridget glimpsed something outside in the woods. First, it was only a shadow. Then she saw the shape of an animal creeping between the trees.

The monster wolf.

She was sure it was him. She felt the grumbling in her stomach again, and she gasped. No, please, *no hiccups*! Not again.

The wolf was moving slowly from one tree to the

other. How come he was still in this area?

She could not say a word or even breathe. She heard her father trying to start the engine again, swearing silently. The wolf sat down, raised his head, and looked at her. Their eyes met. She saw him nodding. At her!

All of a sudden, the van's engine started without a problem. Bridget saw the monster wolf watching them leave. Nobody from her family had seen him, only Bridget.

She watched him until he stood up and vanished back into the woods. She knew she would never see him again in her life.

The maple tree was still standing in the schoolyard when Tom and Bridget entered the gate. Principal Payne stood staring at the tree. When he saw her, he winced.

"Little Miss Knotterfield, what have you *done*?" he said and showed her a piece of paper. "The parents of many kids that go to school here collected signatures to let the tree stay where it is."

Bridget grinned. "But that is wonderful, Principal Payne!"

He was not convinced. "It is, somehow, but . . . well, so . . ."

"So you let it stay," Tom said.

"Well, I think I have to."

Curt arrived carrying a big box, which he opened

with the help of Tom and Bridget. Inside there was a swing set. Principal Payne frowned.

Mandy and Samantha arrived, and they clapped their hands. "Is that for the tree?"

Curt nodded. "Sure!"

Principal Payne said nothing. Instead, he went back inside to prepare for his lessons.

Bridget did not have any more hiccups. Okay— she wasn't called to recite a poem again by Mrs. Peterson, nor to do math at the board. After school, she sat in the nice hammock tree house with Samantha and Mandy and ate cookies. They looked over at the fantasy trees still standing in the grassy field. Mayor Richardson had kept his promise. They had not been removed. Bridget told her friends what happened at Aunt Claire's farm and that they were all new owners of a nice fantasy forest.

"Sound like a ghost story," Samantha said, excited.

"It is not," Bridget assured them. "Since then, I have not had hiccups anymore. But what do you think, shall we go to a fun fair and check it out?"

Her friends looked confused. "What do you mean?"

"Let's try the ghost train!"

But despite screaming herself hoarse in the tunnels, Bridget did not have another hiccup, and she never did again.

However, in the town, she was a special girl to the local people who did not stop believing in magic.

The harp at Nature's advent strung

Has never ceased to play;

The song the stars of morning sung

Has never died away.

John Greenleaf Whittier

STARS SHINE

Are you gloomy sometimes? Of course you are. Do you know anyone who is happy all the time? Probably not.

Jack is nine and he definitely has a gloomy side! One boring afternoon, something strange happens to Jack. He is intrigued by an old man – Mr. Red. Mr. Red is even gloomier than Jack! He tells Jack he is from a distant star – The Shining Star! The spaceship that was intended to take him home has left without him! Jack learns that Mr. Red needs a 'gloom cake' to get home. A gloom cake will grant the wish of anyone who eats it. But a gloom cake has weird, wonderful and very rare ingredients. Did you ever hear of monkeybread-nuts, wonder apples, giggle cherries, balloon melons and fortune peas?

To find those ingredients, the two of them journey to giant trees, a mighty mountain and a mysterious castle at the top of a giant giggle cherry shrub. Are Jack and his strange companion able to prepare the strange gloom cake? Is Mr. Red able to return to his home on The Shining Star?

Read more of this fascinating, gloomy tale to find out!

Illustrated by Bea Balint
114 pages
ISBN 978-1-981044-43-6 Paperback

Thank you...

for joining me on this hiccup fantasy adventure of Bridget and her family. I hope you liked it and enjoyed the story the same way I did.

I want to thank all the people who worked on this book with me: Troon Harrison and Haley Hampton for the English copyediting and proof-reading. Thank you for your ideas! Svetlana Janev did a great job illustrating all my ideas for the story. Thanks to Bea Balint who put the final book into the right shape.

Dear kids,

*If you loved this book and have a minute to spare
I would appreciate your time for a short review on
the page or site where you bought the book, such as
Amazon.com.*

*Your help in spreading the word is greatly
appreciated. Reviews from readers make a
difference and help other children and their parents
find new interesting books to read and discuss.*

*Finally, if you would like to know when my next
book comes out, and want to receive occasional
updates from me, just sign up for my newsletter at*

www.ingoblum.com

*I look forward to your letters, comments, and
opinions.*